WHERE THERE'S A WILL

A GLASS DOLPHIN MYSTERY

JUDY PENZ SHELUK

Superior Shores Press

PRAISE FOR THE GLASS DOLPHIN MYSTERIES

The Hanged Man's Noose (#1)

"A small town with a dark past, its inhabitants full of secrets, a ruthless developer, and an intrepid reporter with secrets of her own come together to create a can't-put-down-read." — *Vicki Delany, bestselling author of the SHERLOCK HOLMES BOOKSHOP mystery series*

A Hole in One (#2)

"A twisty tale chock full of clues and red herrings, antiques and secrets, and relationships that aren't what they seem." — *Jane K. Cleland, award-winning author, JOSIE PRESCOTT ANTIQUES mysteries and MASTERING PLOT TWISTS*

Where There's A Will (#3)

"An intriguing and unputdownable tale of reality TV, real estate, and long-simmering grudges that will leave cozy mystery fans completely satisfied." — *Lois Winston, USA TODAY bestseller and author of the critically acclaimed ANASTASIA POLLACK CRAFTING MYSTERIES*

"In *Where There's a Will*, Judy Penz Sheluk has created a smart mystery with great twists and surprises that will keep you guessing right to the very end." — *Diane Bator, author of the GLITTER BAY, SUGARWOOD, GILDA WRIGHT, and WILD BLUE mystery series*

"The perfect addition to the Glass Dolphin series—classic characters from Lount's Landing, twists and turns, a hint of romance, a real estate bidding war, and a haunted house." — *Susan Van Kirk, bestselling author of the ENDURANCE and SWEET IRON mystery series*

PRAISE FOR THE MARKETVILLE MYSTERIES

Skeletons in the Attic (#1)

"A smartly constructed mystery in the good old-fashioned and highly readable sense." — *Jack Batten, The Toronto Star*

"A thought-provoking, haunting tale of decades-old deception." —*Annette Dashofy, USA Today bestselling author of the Zoe Chambers mystery series*

Past & Present (#2)

"A tense, emotionally gripping, multifaceted mystery that serves both as a perfect continuation of Callie's life story and as a fine stand-alone read for newcomers." — *Midwest Book Review*

"A well-crafted story that keeps readers engaged as history blends into the present." — *Debra H. Goldstein, award-winning author of the Sarah Blair mystery series*

A Fool's Journey (#3)

"A compelling page-turning mystery you won't want to miss." – *Rick Mofina, USA Today bestselling author of The Lying House*

"A well-crafted mystery with fabulous characters and a series of twists and turns that keep you hooked until the end." — *Mike Martin, award-winning author of the Sgt. Windflower mystery series*

ALSO BY JUDY PENZ SHELUK

NOVELS

Glass Dolphin Mysteries

The Hanged Man's Noose

A Hole in One

Where There's a Will

Marketville Mysteries

Skeletons in the Attic

Past & Present

A Fool's Journey

SHORT STORY COLLECTIONS

The Best Laid Plans: 21 Stories of Mystery & Suspense (Editor)

Live Free or Tri

Unhappy Endings

SHORT STORIES

Plan D (The Whole She-Bang 2)

Live Free or Die (World Enough and Crime)

Beautiful Killer (Flash and Bang)

Saturdays with Bronwyn (The Whole She-Bang 3)

Goulaigans (The Whole She-Bang 3)

For my ex-partners in crime at New England Antiques Journal: John, Mary, Mark, Jenn, and Linda

Where There's A Will: A Glass Dolphin Mystery #3

Edited by Ti Locke

Proofread by Jennifer Grybowski

Cover Design by Hunter Martin

Cover Illustration by S.A. Hadi hasan

Published by Superior Shores Press

Four Chapter Preview of Skeletons in the Attic used with permission

ISBN Trade Paperback: 978-1-989495-27-8

ISBN Kindle: 978-1-989495-32-2

ISBN Kobo: 978-1-989495-33-9

ISBN ePub: 978-1-989495-34-6

First Edition: November 2020

1

———

Appraisal Day. Arabella Carpenter was alternately looking forward to and dreading her business partner's latest marketing scheme. Arabella was out of her comfort zone with the project, but it was true that *Antiques Roadshow* and programs like it had large, devoted audiences. Emily wanted to follow Appraisal Day with an "Appraisal of the Week" feature on their website, which seemed like a good idea. But last summer's idea—sponsoring a hole in one contest at a charity golf tournament—had seemed good, too. Unfortunately, it had been a bust; finding a dead body in the woods had a way of putting a damper on things. But Emily Garland assured her Appraisal Day would give the Glass Dolphin the boost it needed.

Keep the lights on was more like it. Folks didn't collect twenty teacups or dozens of Blue Willow platters anymore. In fact, most of those collectors were either dead or downsizing. Unless something was rare and in pristine condition, or truly unique, the market was soft at best, nonexistent at worst. There was a time when "brown" furniture—an antiquer's catchall term for wood—sold well for solid prices. That was until mid-century modern became the latest darling of interior designers and decorator magazines.

Arabella had a sense of what might be trending next, but that wasn't the point. She knew, from her economics classes, that the first two years of any business venture were the most precarious. Getting established meant a lot more than stocking quality inventory and keeping it fresh. There were profit margins to consider, although she'd learned sometimes you were forced to sell something at a loss to pay the rent. That had only happened twice so far, but both times it had stung. And now their landlord was jacking up the rent.

Her know-it-all ex-husband, Levon Larroquette, had warned her about the risks of opening a brick and mortar location on Lount's Landing's historic Main Street. He'd said, "Brick and mortar means overhead and overhead could be the difference between making money or losing it," and that "the idea of breaking even was the cruelest joke of all, giving a shop owner false hope that things would eventually turn around."

The rational side of Arabella knew Levon had a point, but owning her own store had been her dream for as far back as she could remember. She couldn't imagine going back to her nine-to-five job at McLelland Insurance.

An antiques picker since his late teens, Levon had earned a decent living in the past two decades, and he'd taught Arabella most of what she knew. And though she'd remained friends with her ex— and occasionally, if regrettably, more than just friends—she wasn't cut out for the rootless life of a picker.

So here she was, getting ready for the Glass Dolphin's very first Appraisal Day, the doors set to open in under an hour, and where was Emily? Off house hunting. With her fiancé, no less.

◆

Emily felt moderately guilty about not being at the Glass Dolphin for Appraisal Day, but the truth was she was more likely to be a hindrance than any sort of help. Sure, she'd been studying under Arabella for the past few months, but she had miles to go before she would be qualified to offer an appraisal. Her background was in journalism, and her role as partner in the shop was primarily focused on marketing, which was why she'd come up with the

Appraisal Day concept. Arabella had been a reluctant participant at first, but she'd gradually warmed to the idea, albeit with extreme caution. That, to Emily's mind, was Arabella's biggest problem. The woman didn't know how to chill out and have fun. And ever since her short fling with Hudson Tanaka had ended, she'd been broody, too. Would Arabella ever admit to herself that it was Levon or no one?

The break-up with Hudson had caused a few minor ripples in Emily's life. She had recently become engaged to his best friend, Luke Surmanski, but it was nothing they couldn't work around. When the big day came in two months' time, Hudson would be the best man, Arabella the maid—or was it matron?—of honor, and they would all behave like mature adults.

In the meantime, she and Luke needed to find a house of their own, and soon. Emily wasn't about to live in Luke's drafty bachelor flat on top of Luke's Lakeside Marina, even if the view of Lake Miakoda was lovely, and her one-bedroom apartment in Lount's Landing was too small for the two of them. Besides, it was a rental. In Emily's mind, if you got married, you bought a house. End of story.

They'd been house hunting for a couple of months in Cedar County's tri-communities of Lakeside, Miakoda Falls, and Lount's Landing, but nothing had screamed "buy me" to Emily. She didn't want a new build, every house the same as the one next to it. It had to be something older, with character, ideally with Victorian architecture. Not too big, but also not too small, a house large enough to accommodate a family, and a yard with space for a garden—veggies and flowers—a swing set, maybe a wading pool. And it had to be near good schools.

Luke was getting frustrated, as was their realtor, Poppy Spencer, but Emily would know the perfect house when she saw it, and no amount of pressure was going to force her to settle for second-best. This was going to be their forever home, period. She wasn't packing up and moving every time the wind blew in a different direction. She'd moved enough to last her a lifetime.

Even so, she *had* fully intended to be at the Glass Dolphin on

Appraisal Day, until Poppy had called her late the night before, too keyed up to wait until morning. After nearly a decade of being rented out, the old Hadley house was finally on the market. According to Poppy, it was priced to sell and would get snapped up fast.

Emily had hesitated at first, given what she'd heard about the property's history. How many people wanted to buy a house where the owner had been murdered? True, he hadn't actually been murdered in the house, but the case had never been solved, and for the past decade, tenants had come and gone, none staying beyond a few months, most no more than a few weeks. Rumor had it the spirit of Esther Harriet Hadley haunted the house, unable to rest until her husband, Martin's, killer or killers were brought to justice.

Even so, she had to admit that the Hadley house appeared to tick all their boxes, at least from the description and photographs on the agent's website:

Location, location, location! This rustic four-bedroom, two-bathroom Victorian charmer on desirable Walnut Street includes a generous garden for your green thumb and a high-ceilinged lower level with loads of potential. Put your own stamp on this one. Motivated vendor.

Emily had seen enough houses to know that "rustic charmer" translated to "needed serious renovations," whereas the "generous garden for your green thumb" meant an overgrown, weed-infested plot of land, and the "lower level with loads of potential" was realtor speak for an unfinished basement. But the Walnut Street location was absolutely perfect—a ten-minute walk to the Glass Dolphin, and a short drive to reach the main road to Lakeside for Luke. "Buy the worst house on the best street," Poppy had said, and this house certainly qualified.

Prospects and possibilities, that's what a house was supposed to be, not just four walls, a roof, and a place to sleep. Emily browsed through the online photos and virtual tour multiple times, and thought this could be "the one," the creepiness factor of the old murder notwithstanding. Besides, it wasn't as if she believed in ghosts.

2

___

Arabella opened the front door of the Glass Dolphin to find a half dozen people waiting, each one carrying a box, bag, or parcel. It was a promising start, better than she'd expected, and she didn't recognize a single face. New clientele? Maybe this would work out after all.

She welcomed each person, knowing, as she did it, that she was going to need help, if only to manage the store while folks milled about waiting for their turn at the appraisal table set up at the back. It wouldn't do to lose a sale, or heaven forbid, have something stolen from right under her nose. She excused herself, cursed Emily under her breath, and made a quick call to Caitie Meadows, their sometimes shop assistant, who agreed to come right over. Arabella summoned up a bright smile, and, in an effort to kill time before Caitie arrived, gave everyone a quick tour.

"We have a wide selection of antique and vintage merchandise, all strictly vetted, along with some lovely pottery, jewelry, wooden ware, and quilts, handcrafted by local artisans," she was saying as rainbow-haired Caitie strolled in, and she felt the pressure in her chest subside. "Feel free to browse while you wait. Now, who wants to go first?"

There was a bit of shuffling, and after several awkward moments, a young, prematurely balding man stepped forward. Unfortunately, the open-faced pocket watch he thought was old and solid gold was a 1960's gold-plated reproduction. Arabella did her best to break the news gently, pointing out the lack of a carat stamp and the tarnish that wouldn't be there on real gold, but there was no mistaking the disappointment etched on his face. She could feel all eyes on her and knew she had to say more.

"What's your name?"

"Matthew."

"Matthew," Arabella said, her voice soft. "Does this watch have sentimental value?"

Matthew admitted the watch had belonged to his late uncle, and that he had always admired it as a child. He'd done some research on the internet and… His voice had trailed off, the admission bringing a scarlet flush to his cheeks. Arabella wanted to tell him that the internet could be a minefield of misinformation, but that would only serve to embarrass him further. It was better to share some history.

"The reality is, Matthew, even if this one had been vintage, open-face pocket watches were made in tremendous quantities, especially those produced by Elgin or Waltham, like this one. So regardless of the age, there would likely be limited monetary worth, something in the range of a hundred dollars, depending on the model and condition. However, your uncle loved you enough to leave this for you to treasure and remember him by. That makes this very special."

Matthew surprised Arabella by hugging her, and the rest of the folks in the shop clapped. The ice had been broken.

The next object—an intricately carved whale's tooth—was also a fake. Arabella felt sorry for the excited young couple who had discovered their "great find" at a local estate sale, but this wasn't scrimshaw; it was what was known in the business as "fakeshaw," a thermoplastic polymer resin meant to replicate the look of ivory and bone.

The couple, Sal and Sally, had been recording the appraisal on their cell phones, perhaps wishing for a big reveal to post on social media. They turned their phones off and said they had done a "hot needle" test, and the needle couldn't penetrate the bone. Tried a match and it wouldn't burn. That meant it was real, didn't it? That it was bone, not plastic?

"Unfortunately not," Arabella said. "Those tests were useful forty years ago, but, as you can imagine, the makers of fakeshaw changed their formulas to more closely resemble real bone. Even savvy antiques dealers have been fooled. As for this example, if the intention of the maker was to deceive, they have succeeded admirably. Can I ask if this whale's tooth was represented to you as authentic, and did you pay a lot for it? If so, that would be fraudulent and you might have recourse."

Sal and Sally shamefacedly admitted that there had been no claims of authenticity. It was just one of many items at the estate sale, and no, they hadn't paid a lot, about ten dollars, thinking they'd found something truly special. "I suppose we should leave the antiques picking to the experts," Sal said, and Sally had nodded, though she looked close to tears.

"Well, it's worth ten dollars from a decorative standpoint," Arabella said, though as far as she was concerned a fake anything was worthless. But the last thing she needed was a sobbing Sally making everyone else in the shop uncomfortable.

Arabella was grateful the next few items, though neither rare nor valuable, were the real deal. First was a 1960's McCoy Pottery cookie jar in the shape of a golden delicious apple, a chip on the leaf-shaped handle, not that the chip mattered much—the cookie jar collecting craze was firmly rooted in the last century.

Next was a dragon-decorated tea service stamped "Made in Occupied Japan," pretty in its own right, but produced in great quantity during the seven-year allied forces occupation of Japan following the end of World War II. The workmanship was good, but values at auction were almost always less than a hundred dollars.

There was also a complete set of old china with a gold-rimmed scalloped edge and a delicate floral pattern. But even the "Royal" designation in the name didn't give the set any monetary value. No one wanted old dishes any more; they weren't microwavable, you couldn't put them in the dishwasher, and most contained lead-based glazes. A family keepsake to be safeguarded for future generations and used on special occasions was the only way Arabella could spin it.

The day went quickly, the last man and his vintage postcard collection had left five minutes earlier, and with one exception, everyone else, Caitie included, were long gone. The exception was an attractive woman in her late twenties who'd been there since late morning, a canvas bag cradled in her hands. Her hair was long, wavy, and dyed cherry bomb red, a color that shouldn't have worked with her pale complexion, but did. A tattoo of a turquoise-feathered dreamcatcher flowed from mid-thigh to above the knee, a black leather mini dress and leopard print stiletto heels showcasing her well-toned legs.

The woman had watched and listened to every appraisal with unabashed curiosity, her dark eyes taking in every last detail. At first the attention had been flattering, but as the day wore on, it bothered Arabella. There was a hard edge to her, an undercurrent of something Arabella couldn't quite identify, and wasn't sure she'd want to. Her inner instinct told her you wouldn't want to be on the wrong side of this one.

And her inner instinct was seldom wrong.

3

———

THE WOMAN INTRODUCED herself as Faye Everett and apologized for waiting until the end. "I wanted to be sure that you knew your stuff," she said. "Lount's Landing isn't exactly Toronto."

When did Toronto become the gold standard for measuring the worthiness of antiques dealers, Arabella wondered, biting back a snarky response. "I assume I made the grade since you're still here." *Okay, maybe still a little bit snarky.*

Faye blushed. "I deserved that. Let me start over." She pulled a pitted stoneware jug from the canvas bag. "This belonged to my late aunt, and I've always admired it. It has a wonky lean to it, which to my eye makes it a more interesting piece, though unfortunately it's missing the original stopper. I believe at one time there were some old pins inside of it, but they're not there now, and I haven't been able to find them. I assume my aunt tossed them, more's the pity. I was hoping you could tell me something about it."

More's the pity? Arabella would have liked to tell Ms. Everett that her aunt's ignorance bordered on vandalism, but that sort of judgement was best left unsaid. Besides, it was her *late* aunt. It wasn't right to speak ill of the dead. She examined the jug carefully, turning it this way and that, until she knew what it was. Or at least what it used to be.

"What you've got here is a witch bottle. At one time it would have contained handmade pins, rosemary, and…urine." Arabella resisted a chuckle as Faye wrinkled her nose at the mention of urine. "Nicer households might have used wine, but either way, they would have buried the witch bottle under the hearth to capture any evil that happened to get into the house, impale it on the pins, drown it in the liquid, and send it away on the rosemary."

"I've heard of burning sage to cleanse a house of negative energy, but I've never heard of using rosemary. Or pins and urine."

"Burning sage is a ritual called smudging. Its roots are in First Nations cultures and traditions as a way to cleanse negative energies or influences. Rosemary was used by the Greeks and Romans, was believed to grow only in the gardens of the righteous, and was thought to have exorcising qualities that could cleanse people and places of evil spirits. It would be planted around houses to ward off witches, though many believed that if rosemary flourished outdoors it was a sign the woman was boss." Arabella laughed. "There are reports of Colonial husbands sneaking out at night and cutting off the plant's roots so that it would wither and die. Apparently the thought of witches in the house was preferable to a woman ruling the roost."

Faye flashed her first genuine smile of the day. "I expect some modern-day husbands might still feel that way. At any rate, thank you for bringing this object to life for me. In fact, you've done that all day, with every single person who entered the shop. You have a gift."

"Thank you. Were you thinking of selling or consigning the witch bottle?"

"Oh, no, sorry. At least not yet." Faye shook her head. "I'm afraid I've led you astray, though that was not my intention. The real reason I'm here is because of my late aunt. I'm the executrix of her estate. She owned a house on Walnut Street. Quite a nice house, actually, not that she ever lived there or put so much as a penny into it. Rented it since the day she took possession."

Walnut Street. The old Hadley house? It had gotten dilapidated over the years, but Arabella had always admired the architecture. There were rumors it was haunted, but that was just stuff and nonsense.

"Where do I fit in?"

"I've been doing an inventory of the house and found a bunch of stuff in the basement, Christmas ornaments, picture frames, a broken office chair, and based on the dust on everything, no one had set foot in there for years. Regardless, I felt it was my duty to sort out what to put in the garbage and what to donate to charity. I wasn't expecting to find anything of value."

"I'm assuming you did, since you're here."

"Possibly. At the bottom of one of the boxes of ornaments there was an old photograph of a woman reading a book. It has a mirror-like appearance, sort of like a hologram, and it's set inside a hinged leather case with glass on top of the image. I did some online research and I think it could be a daguerreotype, which means it may have some value. I need to hire someone to appraise it and provide as many details as possible. Obviously, we'd have to come to terms that were fair to both of us. "

Arabella felt a stir of excitement. She loved vintage photography, and daguerreotypes were a favorite, something she'd researched to the point of obsession. No matter how much advancement had been made in the digital age, there was something breathtaking about the clarity of a well-shot dag. The words "hire someone to do the appraisal" also had a nice ring.

"I appreciate your vote of confidence, but I must caution you that most daguerreotypes command very little money, even if they're in great condition, and 'reading dags' aren't uncommon." She went to a packed bookcase at the back of the store and pulled out a gold-covered book titled *The Daguerreian Annual 1998: The Official Yearbook of the Daguerreian Society*, and flipped to page 19.

"This article was written by Keith F. Davis, the author of several books on photography, though he is probably best known as the man who built the Hallmark Photographic Collection, which spans the history of American photography. The article is well researched and thorough, and he writes that daguerreotypes with people holding or reading a book are far from rare." Arabella passed the yearbook to Faye and stayed silent as she studied the images, among them, a preacher with a bible, a man with chin whiskers reading, a young girl clutching an open book.

Faye closed the book and handed it back to Arabella, disappointment etched on her face. "I gather this is your way of telling me that you're not interested."

"To the contrary, I'm definitely interested. I just don't want you to spend more on an appraisal than what you might realistically expect to realize at auction. That said, the right provenance can go a long way to escalating value, but that could prove to be very difficult, if not impossible, to ascertain. How detailed do you want me to get?"

"As detailed as you can, right down to including a copy of the article you just showed me, and any others that have merit. I understand and accept that the cost of the appraisal might exceed the value of the daguerreotype, and I can live with that. It's imperative that I have all of my i's dotted and my t's crossed, especially since I'm in line to inherit fifty percent of the estate. The last thing I need is for the will to be contested over some old photograph and wind up with nothing."

"Surely that wouldn't happen."

"I wouldn't bet on it." Faye's expression was dark. "My...the other beneficiary is far from pleased that I'm the one my aunt selected to be in charge. I'm not too stoked about it, either."

"It sounds as if you've been placed into a difficult situation," Arabella said, not wanting to get into the middle of it.

"Difficult?" Faye barked out a hoarse laugh. "My aunt was a widow who never had children, which was a godsend for her unborn, if I'm being completely honest. Knowing her, she's got front row seats to this on-demand performance, and she's enjoying every minute of it, waiting to scare me witless with a sign from above." Faye's dark eyes locked into Arabella's green ones. "Perhaps you knew her? Camilla Mortimer-Gilroy. She used to own the Gilroy Mansion."

4

———————

Arabella chose her words carefully. "It's a small town. You're unlikely to find anyone who didn't know Camilla." *Finding someone who actually liked her, that might be a bit more of a challenge.*

Faye grinned. "It's easy to remain anonymous in Toronto. I imagine it's a lot more difficult in these parts."

"Try impossible," Arabella said. "The thing is, Faye, as much as I'd love the work, I'm not sure I'm the right person to do the appraisal."

"Why not?"

Because Camilla tried to seduce my ex-husband when he wasn't my ex? Maybe did seduce him, despite his claims to the contrary? Arabella took a deep breath. *May as well be upfront with her; she's going to find out any way.*

"Camilla didn't like me very much." *And the feeling was mutual.*

Faye's grin broadened. "Well, she isn't around to complain, is she? But why do I get the sense you're not telling me the full story?"

"Let's just say Camilla had a way of complicating people's lives, mine included."

This time Faye surprised Arabella by laughing out loud. "That was Aunt Cam. If she could find a way to muddy the waters, she'd grab an oar and do it. She's still doing it from the grave, bless her cold, black heart."

"Do I detect a hint of admiration?"

"Maybe a little," Faye admitted. "Aunt Cam always accused me of calling a spade an effing shovel. It's one of the few things we agreed upon. I suspect you're much the same. It's nice to meet a like-minded individual."

Arabella smiled. She'd never heard that expression, but it fit. Still, there was one more thing to discuss. "Once Camilla…er…left Lount's Landing, everyone figured the Hadley house would go up for sale. Instead it sat vacant until…until…"

"You can say it. Until the day she died." Faye shrugged. "What can I say? Cancer tends to be the great equalizer. Ovarian. They don't call it the silent killer for no reason. By the time the doctors diagnosed it she was already stage four. There is no stage five."

"I'm sorry," Arabella said, and was surprised to find out that she actually was. No matter how much chaos Camilla had caused in her life, she'd never once wished her dead. She didn't need the bad karma.

"No need to get maudlin over someone neither of us cared for very much, is there?" Faye said, and Arabella thought, *that's the undercurrent.* She would have to keep her guard up with this one. She suspected that Faye and Camilla were more alike than Faye was willing to admit.

Another thought crossed her mind. "Do you think the daguerreotype belonged to Esther Harriet Hadley?"

"I don't know, but it's unlikely that Aunt Cam ever went into the basement," Faye chuckled. "She'd be annoyed to know that she missed out on something. She claimed to have an interest in antiques, though I expect that designer she hired did most of the buying."

"Shakyra."

"Hmmm?"

"The designer. Her name was Shakyra." Arabella remembered the way Camilla had lorded the whole *Shopping with Shakyra* business over her. So what if the woman had a television show? She couldn't distinguish the real thing from a reproduction—that much had been made abundantly clear when the Gilroy Mansion and its contents had been sold. In fact, she wouldn't be surprised to learn that the piece of fakeshaw had come from there.

"Right," Faye said, interrupting her thoughts. "Shakyra. So, back to the daguerreotype…"

"Did you bring it with you?"

"I'd like you to view it on the premises."

Arabella felt a flash of annoyance. She wasn't about to steal it. "I'd need to know the address."

"I suppose that would help," Faye said with a grin. "It's 21 Walnut."

So it was the old Hadley house, Arabella thought, her annoyance replaced by excitement. She'd always wanted to see the inside, now she'd have her chance, and get paid for the opportunity. "When would you like me there?"

"Does Wednesday morning work for you? Around nine o'clock?"

Emily usually covered Wednesdays, even while house hunting. Worst case, they could ask Caitie to come in for a few hours. "Wednesday morning is perfect."

"Great, because that's the best day for the estate appraiser to come and evaluate the furniture and paintings, along with any of the other contents he might deem worthwhile."

"You've hired an estate appraiser?" Arabella wasn't sure if she should be offended or relieved, though she was leaning towards offended.

"I'm sorry, I should have led with that," Faye said, apologetic. "He came highly recommended, and I didn't want to commission the entire appraisal to one person, considering my situation with the other beneficiary. He's the one who recommended you to research and appraise the daguerreotype, said there was no one better qualified. He assured me you would also be able to work alongside him on the contents for a secondary verification. It's the main reason I wanted you to go to the house."

Could it be…? "What's his name?"

"Levon. Levon Larroquette. I understand you've known each other for some time?"

"You could say that," Arabella said, and shivered, not quite sure why since she wasn't cold. Her mother used to say it meant a goose was walking over your grave. More like Camilla, gloating over it, laughing at the thought of her and Levon working together again. But it was only working on an appraisal together. How complicated could it be?

5

———

Emily met Poppy Spencer at the Hadley house promptly at ten a.m. She was disappointed that Luke wasn't joining them, but they'd seen so many houses together, and he had the marina to run if he wanted to keep it afloat, pun fully intended. If this house truly was "the one," he promised to take it, and her, seriously. Point and promise taken, and the rational side of Emily knew what Luke was saying had merit. This time would be different; she could feel it in her bones.

Poppy fiddled with the lockbox while Emily admired the symmetry of the Victorian architecture. She imagined her and Luke sitting on the porch, a couple of kids playing on the front lawn. They'd be holding hands and…

A black SUV with heavily tinted windows pulled up in front of the house, the engine idling for a moment before being turned off. No one got out.

"I thought we'd be alone," Emily said, disappointed.

"We're supposed to be." Poppy's gray eyes narrowed into slits. "Unfortunately, the executrix hired Bob Wilkes as the listing agent."

Poppy's icy voice made it clear she didn't approve of the change in plans or Bob Wilkes. Arabella had told her Bob and Poppy had been business partners when they'd started out a decade ago, but they'd split up. Poppy joined the RealtyMaxx in town, quickly becoming the agency's top producer, while Bob had started his own independent brokerage.

The last thing she needed was Poppy in a snit, or worse, alienating Bob Wilkes altogether. She was pretty sure that listing agents were bound by a code of ethics to present all offers, but there were shady deals, too bad, too sad for those not in the loop.

"We can view separate areas of the house," Emily said, trying to keep the peace.

Poppy sniffed, then let out a small gasp as a white Mercedes van pulled in behind the black SUV. The words *"Pemberton on Property"* were emblazoned on the side of the van in a rich, royal blue, along with a full color photo of Miles Pemberton, muscular arms crossed in front of a tight white T-shirt, his biceps straining the fabric. A brown leather tool belt was slung provocatively low on his narrow, blue-jeaned hips, and a spotless "P on P" logoed hard hat sat on his head like a fashion statement.

Miles Pemberton hopped out of the van, sleek as a bobcat. At the same time a slender, silver-haired man in his late fifties—he reminded Emily of the actor on Mad Men—climbed out of the SUV. The two men shook hands, conversing quietly, neither one looking at Emily, Poppy, or the house. Pemberton was dressed in jeans, a brown leather bomber jacket, and cowboy boots that had never seen the inside of a barn, let alone a horse. The older man wore a white dress shirt, burgundy-striped silk tie, and a charcoal gray suit that probably cost more than the Glass Dolphin made in a month.

"What's Miles Pemberton doing here, Poppy?" Emily muttered under her breath. "And who's the silver fox with the snazzy SUV?"

Poppy's face was pinched so tight it could have been squeezed into a vice. "The guy with the SUV is Jay Mulacki, a well-known Toronto realtor. To his credit, he actually resembles the headshot on his billboard ads. Botox is my guess. As for Miles Pemberton, I spent the better part of last summer showing him houses. The last time we spoke, he told me his production company had ruled out Lount's

Landing as a possible location. Apparently that's changed and he didn't bother to inform me."

Pemberton on Property was a popular television show featuring Miles, a professional renovator who bought unique homes and then, over the course of a dozen episodes, transformed them for a television audience. His catchphrase, "teachable moments," was the subject of a featured spot in every show. And in each episode, Pemberton would inevitably face an unexpected, and Emily suspected, fabricated—or at least overblown—challenge. In true reality TV fashion, he and his team would always find an innovative and affordable solution to the problem, and the creatively renovated house would go back on the market. It was a formulaic, but entertaining hour, due in large part to Pemberton's charisma on screen, as well as the uniqueness of the homes he featured. Emily had particularly enjoyed the shows featuring an old castle, but this past season had been a bit of a snoozer.

She wasn't enjoying seeing Miles Pemberton now, however, because it meant he was interested in buying this house. How could she and Luke compete with his television budget? Emily could feel her chances slipping away before she'd even had a viewing.

Poppy must have felt her commission slipping away, too, because she strutted over to where the two men were standing, her red-soled Christian Louboutin pumps clicking on the asphalt driveway as she walked.

"*Mr.* Pemberton," Poppy said, heavy emphasis on the "mister." "How nice to see you back in Lount's Landing."

"Poppy." Miles smiled, his amber eyes crinkling at the corners. "So good to see you again. I'm not sure if you've met Jay Mulacki? No? Jay, meet Poppy Spencer. She's one of the tri-county area's top realtors."

"*The* top realtor, Miles," Poppy said, the acerbic intonation evident in every syllable. "I thought I'd hear from you again, considering all the properties we looked at last summer."

"I'm sorry, I should have called you," Miles said, though to Emily's eyes he didn't look in the least bit contrite. Rather, he appeared annoyed at being questioned. He took a step forward, but

Poppy didn't step back. Emily couldn't help but think that Miles Pemberton would never pass Arabella's sniff test when it came to authenticity.

"I'm afraid the fault lies entirely with my production company," Pemberton was saying, his voice slick as silicone. "The network signed an exclusive agreement with Jay for all their real estate holdings. I had no say in the matter."

Emily didn't believe him. He was the CEO of Pemberton Productions and his TV show had been a ratings winner for the past five seasons. She doubted that Poppy did either, not that it mattered. If Miles Pemberton wanted the house, he and his production company would do everything in their considerable power to buy it. She made a vow to never watch another episode of *Pemberton on Property*.

"No say?" Poppy snorted. "Puh-leez, Miles, this isn't my first day in real estate."

Miles shrugged. "The deal with Mulacki is signed, sealed, and delivered, and this property *will* be ours should it fit our mandate. I suggest that you and your client save yourself some time and heartache and get over it. I'm sure there are plenty of other houses that would be suitable."

Get over it? Emily fumed. She wasn't about to hand over the Walnut Street property on a silver platter, and from the hard-set line of Poppy's mouth, neither was her realtor. Miles Pemberton had made sure of that. He'd just made it personal.

6

———————

Emily admitted the house was tired, the hardwood floors under the area rugs in dire need of refinishing, and every wall was covered with flowered paper, but it was nothing some elbow grease and a fresh coat of paint wouldn't fix. Poppy assured her the wall-to-wall furnishings, and an overabundance of what could be loosely described as artwork, would be liquidated before the house was sold. Even better, Poppy said the house used to be a duplex. It would require planning permission, but there was a possibility of converting it back and renting out one side, which would help with the mortgage and additional renovations.

Mindful of the prying eyes and ears of Pemberton and Mulacki, she'd gone outside to call Luke, excited as a five-year-old on her first day of kindergarten. He left the marina straight away, bless his heart, and, upon arrival, went over the place as thoroughly as any home inspector, making notes and doing a lot of hemming and hawing as he opened and closed closets, cupboards, windows, and doors. The furnace was on its last legs, and the central air wasn't much better. The electrical panel needed upgrading, and there was no insulation in the attic to speak of. As for converting it back to a duplex, who knew what you'd find when you started knocking down walls?

Even as Luke made a list of everything that was wrong, Emily was sure he had fallen for the place every bit as hard as she had. The only sour note had been Miles Pemberton. He'd played his cards pretty close to the vest, his expression blandly neutral whenever they'd bumped into him and Jay Mulacki, but Emily, Luke, and Poppy were positive that he was interested in the property. The feeling was reinforced when an attractive redhead in a black power suit met with both men outside, her attitude patently professional. She'd left after a few minutes, but Emily pegged her as someone important. Business partner? Executive producer?

And why wouldn't they be interested? Renovating a house haunted by an unsolved murder would make for great TV. Damn Pemberton. There had to be a way to beat them. There had to be.

That's when Emily came up with the idea. All she had to do was convince Luke and Arabella to go along with it.

✒

EMILY HUSTLED over to the Glass Dolphin shortly before closing time.

"You and Luke want to make an offer on the old Hadley house?" Arabella stared at Emily as if she'd sprouted a third ear in the middle of her forehead.

"The estate isn't accepting offers until next Monday," Emily said, "but, yes, Luke and I are going to meet with Poppy tomorrow to discuss a game plan. Poppy says it's undervalued because of the circumstance surrounding the house."

Arabella wanted to laugh out loud. Trust Poppy to refer to a murder as a "circumstance." Then again, maybe she was being a hypocrite, since she'd just signed a contract with Faye Everett. "If you're sure that's what you and Luke want."

"It is. The only problem is Miles Pemberton."

"Miles Pemberton? The *Pemberton on Property* guy?"

"One and the same. He was there this morning with his realtor, Jay Mulacki."

"I've heard his ads on talk radio," Arabella said. "Buying or selling? Don't trust any old lackey, hire Jay Mulacki."

"Yeah, that's him," Emily said. "Apparently Pemberton's production company has an exclusive deal with him. There was a red-haired woman there as well, first thing in the morning. She only stayed a few minutes, but I had the impression she was part of the television show, maybe a producer or something." Emily began to pace and checked her watch. "Good grief, it's six o'clock already." She went to the front door, locked it, and turned the sign over from Open to Closed. "I need to discuss something else with you, too."

Arabella mentally prepared herself for what was coming because Emily was using the same wheedling tone she'd used to convince her to sponsor the hole in one contest. "Should I pour us a glass of wine?"

Emily smiled. "Why not? And don't forget I want to hear all about Appraisal Day, too."

"You first." Arabella selected two cross-and-olive crystal glasses from a Canadiana pine hutch that handily housed a small wine refrigerator in the bottom cupboard. The wine fridge had been a gift from Emily when they'd become partners. She took out a bottle of her favorite Chilean sauvignon blanc, poured, and handed a glass to Emily. "Cheers."

"Cheers. To our continued partnership, wherever it takes us."

Arabella stopped sipping mid-sip, the already tart wine souring in her mouth. Had she completely misread the situation?

"Are you planning to leave after you get married? Because I didn't think—"

Emily laughed. "Relax, I'm not going anywhere and don't you even consider trying to get rid of me. No, this is actually quite the opposite."

"The opposite? I don't understand."

"Let's go over everything at The Hanged Man's Noose. I have a feeling we're both going to want another drink, and I haven't eaten for hours."

"Come to think of it, neither have I," Arabella said. It wasn't often she forgot to eat, the thought of an order of Betsy's to-die-for Full Noose Nachos had her stomach rumbling. She set down her nearly full wine glass. "Let's go."

IT WAS BUILD-YOUR-OWN taco night at The Hanged Man's Noose, and it was busy. Come to think of it, tacos sounded good, and if she loaded it up with lettuce and tomatoes, it would make her feel as if she was being nutritionally responsible. Emily, a vegetarian, might approve, though she'd only recently kicked a lingering addiction to bacon.

They found a table for two near the back, beneath a neon Labatt's Blue sign, one of the few modern touches in the nineteenth-century salon-style décor. Betsy Ehrlich, Arabella's longtime friend and the Noose's owner, waved at them enthusiastically, a wide smile crossing her gamin-like face. She was wearing what Arabella had come to think of as her uniform: a black turtleneck, black leggings, black leather over-the-knee boots, and a blood red apron. Her dark brown hair had been twisted back into a bun, revealing diamond-studded ears and a long, thin neck with a pink butterfly tattoo behind her left ear. She slid up to their table, two menus in hand.

"Thanks for coming in. How was Appraisal Day?"

Arabella grinned. "I'm still trying to decide on the correct adjective. I'll fill you in when you're not as busy." She looked around the room. "The taco night idea seems to be taking off."

"For now, anyway. I'm planning to implement a different theme for each night of the week. Taco Tuesdays, Wednesday wings, Thursday two-for-one Treasontinis, Friday fish fry…you get the idea."

The Treasontini was the bar's signature drink, a mix of blueberry juice, blueberry vodka, triple sec, and a splash of club soda. Good, but a bit too sweet for Arabella's taste. They spent a couple of minutes chatting about the pros and cons of theme nights and then ordered: two glasses of house white, beef tacos for Arabella, and a bowl of spicy black bean chili with a side of Mexican bruschetta for Emily.

Arabella waited until Betsy came back with their wine before getting down to business.

"You said something like 'to our continued partnership, wherever it takes us,'" Arabella said. "If you're not leaving, then what exactly are you planning?"

"Well, it's not exactly a plan." Emily began shredding her paper napkin. "The thing is, both Luke and I love the Hadley house, but it needs a new furnace and AC, insulation in the attic, an updated electrical panel, and a ton of cosmetic work. I'm not sure we can swing doing the necessary renovations and make the mortgage payments. And then there's the possibility of a bidding war. There's an open house on Sunday, and the owner isn't accepting offers until Monday, so even if Pemberton isn't interested—and I'm sure he is—there could be other offers as well. Poppy warned Luke and I of that possibility, which means we have to come in above the asking price."

"Where do I come in?" Arabella asked.

Emily stopped fidgeting with her napkin and smiled. "We thought you might want to go in with us, as a co-owner."

Arabella stared at her friend. The wedding must really be doing a number on her head if Emily thought this would be a good idea. "You want me to move in with you and Luke? I'm all for being partners but that might be a bit cozy."

"Not in with us, per se." Emily explained the possibility of converting the house back to a duplex, with Arabella owning one side, she and Luke the other. "You're always complaining about how your midtown rental lacks character, and how much you hate paying your landlord's mortgage. This house has plenty of character, you'd be building your own equity, and it's a hop, skip, and a jump to the Glass Dolphin. It's a win-win-win."

A win-win-win? Arabella wasn't so sure about that. The work and legalities involved in the renovation seemed daunting at best and impossible at worst, but much of what Emily said was true. Her midtown apartment did lack character and she *was* tired of paying her landlord's mortgage. But did she really want to live next door to her business partner?

Arabella was still mulling over Emily's proposal when Betsy arrived with their food and a generous supply of napkins. "Let's drop the subject until I've had a chance to process the pros and cons."

"I've already thought about those. Pro…."

"You nattering on doesn't help me think."

"I don't natter," Emily said, but she made an elaborate gesture of sealing her lips and throwing away the key.

7

———

ARABELLA FILLED EMILY in on Appraisal Day while they ate dinner, leaving out the part about Faye Everett until after they'd finished eating. Hopefully an opening would present itself so it wouldn't seem as if she'd been holding back.

"It sounds like you had quite the day," Emily said. "Do you think it was worthwhile?"

"It depends on your definition of worthwhile. I would definitely consider holding another one. I didn't have an *Antiques Roadshow* moment, but I think everyone who came walked away thinking good things about the Glass Dolphin. I made sure to get the contact information from everyone who attended, so we can follow up with a personalized thank you."

"Good thinking. What if we included a discount coupon code to be used on any one item we have posted online? We could also offer a coupon to be used in-store."

Arabella considered the idea. "I think it's worth a try. How does fifteen percent sound?"

"I was thinking more along the lines of twenty percent. Why don't we test drive it and see if it generates any sales? Fifteen for online and twenty percent in-store."

"I can live with that."

"I'll get on it first thing tomorrow." Emily sighed, her expression bleak. "I truly believed an Appraisal Day would result in money coming in, not just goodwill. I'm sorry it didn't work out that way."

It was the opening Arabella needed. "Actually, it did result in a job."

Emily's expression brightened. "Do tell."

"A woman came into the shop mid-afternoon," she began, and continued with the story, studiously ignoring Emily when she went back to shredding her napkin. She wrapped up the narrative, forcing a sunny smile. "So the day wasn't a complete bust from a financial standpoint. Of course, it will mean working with Levon again, at least for a few hours."

"How could you?" Emily's voice trembled with rage.

"How could I what? Work with Levon again? I'll admit things have been strained between us, but we're both adults and—"

"How could you let me blather on about buying the Hadley house, knowing you had already signed a contract to appraise the contents?" Emily shoved the remnants of her napkin into her empty wine glass, and started on another. "What are the terms of the contract?"

"Standard terms at fifty dollars an hour. My primary responsibility is to provide an in-depth appraisal of a daguerreotype, assuming that's what it is, along with any history I might find. Other than that I'm expected to confirm Levon's appraisal, or offer an alternate point of view if I think one is required. There's an issue with the other beneficiary and—"

"Yes, but what exactly does it *say*?" Emily asked, interrupting again. "Does it say, 'Arabella Carpenter will' or does it say, 'Arabella Carpenter on behalf of the Glass Dolphin will?' It's an important distinction."

"It says the *Glass Dolphin* will, and naturally the income would go into our gross revenue. We're partners. I wouldn't dream of leaving you out of it."

"Yet you signed the contract without any thought of discussing it with me."

"The hourly rate is more than fair, and it's not like we can't use the money. I was actually quite pleased with my negotiating skills."

"Were you, now?"

Arabella watched Emily attack another napkin. At this rate, Betsy would have to haul out the shop vac. "I don't understand why you're getting so bent out of shape over this. I've already assured you that the Glass Dolphin, and by extension, you, are being treated in an equitable manner."

"I'm thinking of the potential ramifications."

"What potential ramifications?"

"I'm not a lawyer, but what if by being part of the appraisal team we're precluded from putting in an offer?"

"Why on earth would that happen?"

"Don't you see?" Emily said, her lower lip quivering. "Miles Pemberton can say we have an unfair advantage. It's just the sort of thing he would pull."

"An unfair advantage? Why?"

"Because by taking on the appraisal, we're no longer arm's-length bidders. By the time we are, he'll own the Hadley house."

"I think arm's-length only refers to tax implications when a house is being sold to family members, so the house is sold at fair market value," Arabella said. "I don't think it matters that the Glass Dolphin is doing the contents appraisal."

"Are you sure?"

"Pretty sure," Arabella said, though in truth she had no idea. "Anyway, how was I to know you and Luke were looking at the house? You didn't mention which house you were going to look at today."

Emily rolled her eyes. "Poppy called me late and I didn't get a chance. And at least I talked to you before making a decision that would impact your life."

Arabella knew Emily was being unreasonable, but she still wished she'd listened to her gut before signing on the dotted line.

Her gut.

"You said that a red-haired woman was there with Pemberton and Mulacki. Can you describe her and what she was wearing?"

Emily nodded. "Sure. Pale complexion, hair done up in a French braid. Attractive with a bit of a hard edge. Black blazer, black dress pants, low-heeled leather pumps, white silk blouse, pearl drop earrings. Her hair color was the only thing about her that wasn't conservative. It was fire-engine-red, nothing you'd ever find in nature, but it suited her."

Fire engine red hair. Could the woman Emily had seen at the Hadley house be Faye Everett? If so, why try to alter her appearance? Why hire Arabella and the Glass Dolphin to do the appraisal rather than a Toronto firm? Why offer fifty dollars an hour when twenty-five was the going rate?

There was only one answer, and it wasn't because Faye Everett had been swayed by Arabella's expertise. She had hired them so they couldn't put an offer in on the Hadley house. The question was, why?

"There's something else I need to tell you," Arabella said.

⬥

"Let me get this straight," Emily said, once Arabella finished. "You think the woman I saw at the Hadley house is Faye Everett, the same woman who hired the Glass Dolphin to do the appraisal."

"I think it's a strong possibility, but there's one way to be sure," Arabella said, thankful that they'd installed a security camera in the shop. She hadn't liked the idea, initially, considering it an invasion of their customers' privacy, but it had been all but impossible to obtain affordable insurance without one.

"We can check the digital files," Emily said, one step ahead of her. "Let's pay our tab and go back now."

Arabella wanted nothing more than to relax in a hot bubble bath with a good book before heading off to bed, but there'd be no relaxing or sleeping until they were certain. She motioned Betsy for their bill and got ready to head back to the Glass Dolphin.

⬥

It took several minutes and a few tries for Arabella to get to the time code with Faye Everett in the frame. "I know it's black and white, so the hair isn't easily recognizable, but could this be the same woman you saw at the Hadley house?"

Emily studied the screen. "She's dressed differently, and her hair is loose instead of being twisted into a French braid, but it looks like the same woman. There's something that's bothering me, though. How would she have known that I was associated with the Glass Dolphin? Maybe her coming here and hiring us was a coincidence."

"My guess is Bob Wilkes told Mulacki that you were interested. He probably made it sound like the Glass Dolphin was a thriving enterprise, that as co-owner you'd be up for a bidding war. That could also explain why Mulacki and Pemberton were viewing the property at the same time. It was a pressure tactic orchestrated by Wilkes."

"I suppose that's possible," Emily conceded. "So what do we do now?"

"Not we. Me. I'm going to come right out and ask her. I'm meeting her at the Hadley house Wednesday at nine."

"I'd like to come with you, as your business partner. We can ask Caitie to cover for us."

"I think it's better if I go alone. The minute Faye sees you she'll know that we know. I'd rather catch her off-guard."

"I can't say I love the idea of staying behind, but you're probably right."

"That's the spirit. And Emily, don't give up hope. There might still be a way to put in an offer. We have until Monday to figure it out. That gives us five days."

Emily smiled. "Us? Are you saying you'd be willing to partner with Luke and I?"

"Let's just say I'm considering it, though I'm not sure if it's because I think it's a good idea or because I don't like the idea of Pemberton and company pushing you out. Now come on. It's time to get out of here and head on home. I have a hot bubble bath calling my name."

8

FAYE EVERETT WAS WAITING outside the Hadley house when Arabella arrived a few minutes before nine. Once again, Faye's red hair hung loose down her back in waves, though she'd replaced the leather mini-dress with jeans and a Toronto Raptors T-shirt, and the leopard print stilettos with well-worn sneakers. The outfit softened her edge, making her look younger, more vulnerable. There was no sign of Levon's pickup.

"You're punctual," Faye said. "I like that."

"You'd love my partner, Emily Garland, then," Arabella said. "She was a journalist in her former life, always on deadline. If she's on time she considers herself ten minutes late."

"I'd like to meet her."

A perfect opening. "I think you already have."

Faye wrinkled her brow. "Was she in the Glass Dolphin on Appraisal Day? What does she look like?"

Should she tell her Emily wasn't there? Or describe her and gauge Faye's reaction?

Arabella opted for the latter. "Athletic looking with a runner's body. Mid-thirties, shoulder-length dark brown hair, usually tied back in a ponytail, hazel eyes flecked with gold. She's pretty in a natural, girl-next-door sort of way."

"I don't remember her," Faye said, her eyes narrowed in concentration. "It's possible that she left before I got to the store."

"Actually, she wasn't there."

"Then I don't understand. Why would you think I've already met her?"

"Because she was house hunting."

"Okay…I still don't understand how I know her."

"She was here on Monday for a viewing with her realtor, Poppy Spencer. She was expecting to view the property on her own, but Bob Wilkes double booked the tours. Emily saw you here with Jay Mulacki and Miles Pemberton."

"That bitch," Faye said, smashing her hand against the front door. "That bloody bitch."

Arabella felt her face flush with anger, but she managed to keep her emotions in check and her voice controlled "I hardly think viewing a house that's for sale qualifies Emily as a bitch. If you think that, then I think you've found the wrong appraiser. Which, quite frankly, you probably have if you think your little maneuver will preclude her or us from placing a bid."

"Placing a bid? On the property?" Faye's look of bewilderment seemed real, but before Arabella could comment, Faye said, "I'm sorry. I didn't mean to imply Emily was a bitch. I meant that my half-sister, Megan the Manipulator, was a bitch."

Megan the Manipulator? Now it was Arabella's turn to be confused. "Your half-sister? Is she the other beneficiary?"

"One and the same. Aunt Camilla was our father's sister, not that they ever got along. Oil and water, those two. Megan is his daughter from his second marriage. We're often mistaken for each other, though Megan is two years younger than me. From a personality standpoint, we're polar opposites. We grew up in very different households."

So it was Megan, not Faye, that Emily had seen. But something in Faye's tone gave Arabella pause. As curious as she was to know more, this was no time to ask what made the households so different. It was clear, however, that there was no love lost between Faye and her half-sister. Interesting, too, that they had both dyed their hair a vibrant shade of red. Arabella wondered who had copied whom, and what point they were trying to make. Because Arabella was sure there was a point.

"What is Megan's relationship with Miles Pemberton?"

"She's the executive producer of *Pemberton on Property*, and last I heard she was also developing a new series called *Barn Stars*." There was more than a trace of bitterness in Faye's voice. "She's quite a rising star, always manages to be in the right place at the right time, and if she's not, she pushes aside anyone who was there first."

"I take it *Barn Stars* was your idea?"

Faye nodded. "I was foolish enough to tell her about the concept. It's about a twenty-something couple that travels across the country restoring dilapidated barns. She pitched the idea to the network before I could. Took full credit, never mentioned my name. Of course, in true Megan form, she didn't tell me. I found that out *after* I made my pitch to the suits. I'm not sure what was more humiliating, my naiveté trusting Megan or their reaction to me prattling on."

"I'm sorry," Arabella said, not sure what else to say.

"I should have known better. Megan never played fair, even when we were kids. Of course, my father didn't help. He lavished her with praise and the finest things money could buy, while my mom fought for child support and bought my clothes in thrift shops. But enough about that. You were asking what Megan's relationship was with Miles Pemberton. Insider gossip says *Pemberton on Property* is on the chopping block unless the ratings improve. The scuttlebutt is last season was too predictable." Faye grimaced. "He's handsome, debonair, and without any moral compass. I'm not sure what those two have cooked up, but your friend Emily will be in for a tough go of it should Miles decide he wants this place. In fact, if he suspects that Emily is even remotely interested, it will be enough to spur him on to win at any cost."

Definitely spoken as a woman scorned, or at least burned. "But surely, as the executrix, you'll have a say over what offer gets accepted?"

"You'd think so, but no. The will stipulates that both Megan and I must be in agreement, although we can allow a third party to intervene in the event of a stalemate. Because my relationship with Megan is toxic, I suggested that the bank oversee all offers. The estate lawyer concurred and even Megan agreed it was for the best." Faye gave a bitter laugh. "I was grateful that we agreed on something. Of course, learning of Pemberton's interest in the property explains Megan's unexpected acquiescence."

"I don't understand. What does one thing have to do with the other?"

"Don't you see? If the bank oversees the bidding process, there's no way any bidder can claim undue influence."

Emily would be glad to hear it, Arabella thought, as Levon's pickup truck pulled into the driveway.

LEVON HOPPED out of the truck and shambled up to the porch. He had a few more gray streaks in his shaggy brown hair, and he'd grown a beard since the last time she saw him, but he was dressed in his usual head-to-toe denim, the blue bringing out the indigo of his eyes. And, he looked good. Better than good.

From the infatuated look on Faye's face, Arabella wasn't the only one who found Levon attractive. It annoyed her that she was a little bit jealous. Which was ridiculous. Her romantic relationship with Levon was done, done, and done again.

Wasn't it?

Of course it was, and no amount of cognac was going to change things this time. But that didn't mean they couldn't work together, maybe even become platonic friends again. She walked around the carrying case that held her equipment, summoned up a smile, and held out her hand. "Levon, it's been too long."

Levon ignored her hand and gave her a hug, murmuring into her ear. "Your choice, not mine, Bella baby. By the way, you look amazing."

Arabella pulled away, her face flushed. Faye was studying them both, an impish grin on her face.

"You two really do go a ways back, don't you?"

"We used to be married, but don't worry, working together won't be a problem," Levon said. "We still like each other."

Faye's grin widened. "So it would seem. Come on then, let's get inside. It's time to get started."

9

———————

Emily was in a foul mood, and not just because she'd woken up with a nasty cold. If you had the flu, everyone sympathized with you. A cold, not so much. You were expected to get on with your day, which was why she hadn't called Caitie to fill in for her at the Glass Dolphin.

Still, it wasn't the cold that had set her off as much as the latest entry in that annoying blog, *Outside the Landing*. The blog was written anonymously by someone who called themselves Truth Seeker—an oxymoron if there ever was one. Emily was certain the person behind the blog was her old nemesis, Kerri St. Amour, currently the editor of the local paper, *Inside the Landing*. Of course, Kerri couldn't write libelous claptrap in a newspaper and expect not to get sued. *Outside the Landing* solved that problem. She wrote straight-up news stories in the paper and malicious gossip in the blog. The online world was full of trolls; one more wouldn't make much difference.

Emily knew she could ignore the blog, but folks in town talked about it. A lot. Ignoring *Outside the Landing's* rumors and innuendos meant you were out of the loop. And Truth Seeker had targeted her, Arabella, and the Glass Dolphin on more than one occasion. It had become part of her morning routine to check the blog for new posts right after she read her horoscope. Not that she really believed in horoscopes, though she did have the loyal, sensitive, creative, and inquisitive nature of a Cancerian. Okay, and maybe she could be a wee bit moody, too.

Today's horoscope had warned her to "Be prepared for unexpected news and to avoid confrontations with strangers or risk harming her reputation." Phooey. It would have been nice to have an upbeat message. The warning only served to increase her already dour mood.

Today's post in *Outside the Landing* did nothing to improve her spirits.

Boo! The old Hadley house is on the market after years of rentals and reports of Esther Harriet Hadley's spirit still roaming the premises. Word on the entertainment street has it that handsome MILES PEMBERTON is planning to purchase the house, but not for his ailing—or is that FAILING?—television show, PEMBERTON ON PROPERTY. Rumor has it that Pemberton's newest project will be titled HOUSE HAUNTERS. Coincidence? I think not. You read it here first!

Emily was certain the anonymous source was Pemberton, trying to spook anyone who might be interested, not that she could prove it. She tried calling Poppy, got her voicemail, and hung up without leaving a message.

❧

EMILY STOOD in line at Dollars to Donuts, trying not to sniffle, snuffle, or sneeze, a bag of natural herb cough drops in one hand, a box of facial tissues in the other. She'd popped over to the dollar store, leaving a "Back in 5" sign in the front window of the Glass Dolphin, thinking it would be a quick trip. No such luck. With only one cashier on duty, and shoppers with carts filled to the brim with boxes of chocolate, candy, and holiday decorations, the lineup was almost out the door.

Hopefully the cough drops, which included vitamin C and were billed as an immune system support supplement, would get her through the day. She tucked the cough drops and tissue box under her left arm, cursing herself for not picking up a basket, and fished around in her purse for something to wipe her nose, only to come up empty. She thought about opening the box she had yet to purchase but ended up wiping her nose on her coat sleeve, hoping no one would notice. With this cold, couldn't even go for a run tonight to burn off the house-hunting stress.

Emily was finally next in line, her already limited patience tried as the customer in front of her hemmed and hawed over whether or not to buy a three-dollar wreath. She felt like handing the woman three bucks just so she could get out of the store.

Another cashier ambled up from the back of the store. "I'll take the next person in line," she called out in a monotone voice. Emily debated staying put or winding her way over where a tall man at the tail end of the lineup charged forward. She hated it when people butted in.

"She asked for the *next* person in line." Emily stomped over and attempted to position herself in front of him.

"You snooze, you lose," the man said. "Besides, I'm in a hurry."

"And I'm not?" Emily said and glanced at the cashier, hoping for an intervention, only to find her studiously staring at the floor. She could feel the eyes of the other customers upon them, and knew, as a shop owner on Main Street, that she should be the adult in the room and let the man go ahead. She was about to do just that when she recognized the man beneath his sunglasses, scarf, and baseball cap.

Miles Pemberton. It was bad enough that he planned to beat her out of the Hadley house, now he was trying to beat her in line. Well, too bad, too sad, it wasn't going to happen.

"We're all in a hurry, and you are being incredibly rude. Now if you'll excuse me, I believe I'm ahead of you."

"And I believe that you've mistaken me for someone who cares." Pemberton placed a four-pack of AA batteries on the counter. Emily watched as the cashier, the gutless wimp, made a motion to ring him in.

"No." Emily grabbed the batteries out of the cashier's hand and slammed her cough drops onto the scanner. "I'm first."

There were a few audible gasps and the sound of footsteps as customers headed back to the other lineup. Emily knew she was behaving like an idiot, but she couldn't stop herself.

"Now who's being incredibly rude?" Pemberton asked.

"You are," Emily said, and it was all she could do not to wipe the smirk right off his too-handsome face. Just because he had a reality TV show didn't mean he could bully his way through life.

"That'll be two-fifty," the cashier said, saving Emily from doing or saying something else she was bound to regret. She handed over a toonie and two quarters and made a beeline for the door, eyes averted, her face flushed with embarrassment, hoping that no one had filmed the exchange. Wouldn't that make a juicy tidbit for *Outside the Landing?*

She was about to enter the Glass Dolphin when Pemberton's voice rang out from behind her. "So this is where you work."

Emily spun around, feeling slightly intimidated. "You're stalking me?"

"Don't flatter yourself," Pemberton said with a guttural laugh. "I recognized you from the Hadley house. You were there with Poppy Spencer, all puppy-eyed and pathetically eager. It's going to be great fun bidding against you. I guarantee you, I'm going to win."

He was gone before Emily could think of a witty retort, which was just as well. She'd caused herself quite enough trouble for one day. That's when she remembered her horoscope. Maybe there was something to those, after all.

Wallpaper. That's the first thing Arabella noticed when she walked into the Hadley house. A pattern of pink cabbage roses, intermingled with tendrils of ivy, covered every wall. Paintings and portraits hung everywhere, most clashing with the wallpaper. Still, there were a few nice pieces of furniture, including an oak dining room table and matching sideboard, a pair of stacking bookcases filled with an assortment of leather-bound volumes, and a phenomenal rolltop desk. Desks in general didn't sell as well as they used to—they weren't considered ergonomically friendly for today's computer user—but Arabella could tell this one was special. The way Levon's eyes were drawn to it confirmed her impression.

"I wanted to declutter before listing the property," Faye said, "but Megan wouldn't hear of it. She felt it gave the place ambience. I considered removing some of the paintings, but the wallpaper has faded." She laughed. "You think the wallpaper's bright now, wait until you see what it looked like new."

"It's hard to believe Camilla rented the house out with all of this stuff inside," Levon said. "Usually rental properties are stripped to the bare bones, even when they're advertised as fully furnished.

Camilla was a shrewd businesswoman without a sentimental bone in her body. I'm surprised she didn't sell the lot of it."

Arabella had been thinking the same thing. It was no wonder tenants had felt the presence of Esther Harriet Hadley when they'd lived here. It was like walking into a time capsule.

"She might have, but Uncle Graham wouldn't hear of it, and he'd owned the house before they were married." Faye said. "Even his will contained explicit instructions to leave everything in the house as Esther had left it, unless, and only unless, Camilla made it her primary residence." Faye laughed. "As if Aunt Cam would have ever considered moving here. It's a lovely street and the house has good bones, but it's a considerable step down from the Gilroy Mansion. My uncle would have counted on that."

Graham Gilroy had died when his snowmobile fell through thin ice on the Dutch River, though whether he died from hypothermia or drowning had been the subject of hot debate. Some folks had even hinted that Camilla might have had a hand in his premature demise; rumors that the couple's marriage had been in trouble rumbling amongst town circles. But when Graham's impending bankruptcy came to light—and that he'd had twice the legal limit of alcohol in his system—even the most avid Camilla detractor had to admit it sounded more like suicide than murder. But none of that explained why he wanted things in the house left as is.

"I wonder why Graham cared," Arabella said.

"Perhaps the reason will be revealed when I go through everything." Levon walked over to the desk, his hands caressing the polished oak surface. "Who knows what secrets this might hold?"

"Ah…the desk. That might pose a problem," Faye said. "I can't find a key. Scoured the kitchen cupboards, the wardrobe in the basement—it was a bit creepy going through Esther's old clothes, let me tell you—but despite my best efforts, I didn't find it. I thought about hiring a locksmith or picking the lock myself but I'd probably damage the desk before I got the lock open. And it seems wrong."

Arabella understood exactly where her Faye was coming from. A desk as fine as this deserved respect, as did any secrets it might contain.

Levon cast a sideways glance at Arabella. "Maybe I'll get lucky."

It was common to tape a key to the back or underside of a desk, and Arabella knew it would be the first place Levon would look. So why did his "get lucky" make her blush? Annoyed at her reaction, she leveled him with her best steely-eyed stare and addressed Faye.

"And maybe there's something inside Graham didn't want Camilla to find. Like the daguerreotype. Knowing Camilla, she would have sold it without a second thought, the as-is clause notwithstanding. Something that small, no one would notice it missing."

"To be fair, we don't even know if Uncle Graham was aware it existed," Faye said. "I found it in the basement, inside a box of Christmas ornaments." She opened the sideboard and pulled out a somewhat battered cardboard box with the Shiny Brite logo and an old-fashioned graphic design of a Christmas tree. "It's inside here. I thought you could work at the kitchen table."

"Sounds like a plan," Arabella said, keen to get started, not to mention out of Levon's sight. She took the box and made her way to the kitchen.

11

———

Faye slipped into the kitchen behind Arabella. "Do you mind if I join you?"

Arabella felt a flush of anger. She hadn't even opened the box yet. "This arrangement won't work if you don't trust me."

"Oh my gosh, no. That's not why I wanted to join you. I'd like to learn more about daguerreotypes in general."

"Let me take a quick look first," Arabella said, studying the daguerreotype from every angle. As was customary, it was housed in a leather case, somewhat worn but still intact, the delicate mirrored surface further protected by glass.

The portrait was of an attractive young woman, an enigmatic smile on her face. Her hair had been parted in the center, then carefully braided and twisted into small buns on either side of her head, not quite *Star Wars* Princess Leia, but close. The dress was clearly a "Sunday best" with a lace collar and black velvet ribbon at the neck, and scalloped edges on the sleeves. She held a half-open book on her lap, the title too tiny to make out.

"It's in great shape overall, no damage outside of slight wear to the case," she said to Faye. "This particular example, referred to as a sixth-plate, the most common size, measures 2.75 by 3.25 inches.

Full plates, 6.5 by 8.5 inches, are the least common. As for the subject matter, it's definitely a reading daguerreotype, but I wasn't expecting the subject to be so charming."

"A common size, in great shape, with a charming subject," Faye said. "So far, so good. But what can you tell me about daguerreotypes in general?"

"I'd love to share the history," Arabella said with a smile. "In 1827, a French inventor, Nicéphore Niépce, produced the world's first photograph, taken on an asphalt-coated pewter plate. Unfortunately, his efforts went largely unrecognized and his photographic process, with an exposure time of over eight hours, was impractical."

"Eight hours for one photograph?"

Arabella chuckled. "It's hard to believe when we can snap a selfie in seconds with a smartphone. Anyway, at the same time, Louis Daguerre, a French commercial artist, had been working on making the images, seen through a camera obscura, permanent."

"Camera obscura?" Faye asked.

"Simply put, it's a darkened enclosure, something like a duck blind, in which images of outside objects can be projected onto a facing surface."

"Clear as mud," Faye said, "but go on."

"Daguerre promised to improve Niepce's process, and the two men signed an agreement in 1829. Unfortunately Niepce died in 1833 without seeing any improvements to his photography."

"I'm guessing Daguerre didn't give up."

"Not for a moment, though his discovery *was* the result of an accident. In 1835 an exposed silver-coated copper plate had acquired an image after lying in his chemical cupboard overnight. Further investigation revealed the fumes from a broken mercury thermometer had been responsible for the transformation. Two years later, Daguerre succeeded in making the images permanent by immersing the plates in a solution of cooking salt. He tried to sell licenses for his new invention, but in the nineteenth century the idea of mercury fumes creating images visible only under a dark cloth was incomprehensible."

"It's still incomprehensible," Faye said. "Especially because we now know the dangers of breathing mercury. But weren't daguerreotypes hugely popular? He must have sold the idea to someone."

Arabella nodded. "He had one fan, Francois Argo, a respected member of the Academy of Sciences. Argo convinced the French government to compensate Daguerre directly, and in 1839 the daguerreotype was announced before the Academy of Sciences and publicized as France's gift to the world. In 1840, the daguerreotype process was simplified by an improved camera, which reduced the exposure time. It's important to note, however, that Daguerre's process was discovered around the same time as England's William Fox Talbot introduced a photographic method using a negative."

"Surely the negative outweighed the daguerreotype," Faye said.

Arabella shook her head. "You'd think so, and the use of negatives in photography would eventually become the norm, but in 1840's and 50's America, the daguerreotype had little competition, especially in the area of private portraiture. Every town had at least one daguerreotype studio. There were also itinerant photographers who traveled in horse-drawn carriages in the tradition of the traveling salesman or portrait-painter. By 1850, there were more than ten thousand daguerreotypists in the United States alone. Before this, portraits and miniatures were considered luxuries for the rich. Suddenly, middle class America had a chance to have their pictures taken. By 1853, *The New York Daily Tribune* estimated that three million daguerreotypes were being made annually."

"Three million every year," Faye said, a look of disappointment crossing her face. "And here I hoped this one would be special."

"We don't know that it isn't…yet. For one, daguerreotypes are easily damaged, and damage greatly diminishes the value. For another, the subject matter and provenance is paramount. There are collectors who only collect occupational dags…men posed with the tools of their trade or goods that they have made, such as cobblers, carpenters, or blacksmiths. Others specialize in dog dags."

"Dog dags?"

"Even in the nineteenth century, dog owners would happily pay to have a photo taken with Fido, even if that meant giving the dog a shot of whiskey to keep him calm for the photo shoot. Cats were another popular subject. But the most valuable dags usually have historical significance."

"You know," Faye said, the sparkle back in her eyes, "daguerreotypes might be a great subject for a made-for-TV documentary."

Arabella was momentarily taken aback. Was that what Faye's interest was all about? A way to get back at Megan for *Barn Stars*? "You produce documentaries too?"

"Reality TV has a bigger market than intelligently researched and produced content," Faye admitted. "But I think we can sell it, especially with the backstory on this reading dag."

"We?"

"Yes, we. You don't think I could do this without you, do you?" Faye clapped her hands. "Trust me. It's going to be perfect."

Trust her? Arabella barely knew Faye, and she certainly didn't know anything about writing for television. "First, it's unlikely this dag will be special enough to garner television interest. Second, I'm not sure if I'm the right person for the job."

"You're the perfect person for the job." Levon stood in the doorway, hands on hips, a wide grin on his too-handsome face.

"I thought you were appraising the furniture and paintings," Arabella said.

"I was in the next room. I couldn't help but overhear. You have to do it. You'll be doing the research anyway and you can always provide Faye with information about more famous dags to spice things up. Imagine the free publicity it will bring the Glass Dolphin."

In Arabella's experience nothing in life was ever truly free. There was also Emily's earlier outrage to consider. "I'd have to run the idea by Emily."

"I wouldn't have it any other way," Faye said.

"And there'd need to be a contract."

"Goes without saying."

"I assume you'll need to discuss this with Megan and the network executives first."

"Until the script is written and I'm ready to pitch the idea, I have no intention of mentioning this to anyone else. As for Megan Sutcliffe, she will be the last to know."

The hatred in Faye's voice when she said Megan Sutcliffe was evident in every syllable. Arabella wondered what event or events had occurred to merit such toxicity. She looked up at Levon, wishing that she didn't care quite so much about his opinion. He was nodding at her, urging her to go for it. She found herself nodding back. Maybe Emily could even help with the writing.

But first this daguerreotype would have to tell the rest of its story.

❦

ARABELLA OPENED her bag and removed a camera, black cloth, and small rectangular box made of black foam board, a small hole punched in the middle. "In order to research this properly back at the Glass Dolphin, I'm going to need several good quality photographs," she told Faye, fussing with the settings on her recently purchased DSLR camera. She'd second-guessed the expenditure, money being tight, but it would prove invaluable now. Smartphones and tablets were okay, but this job depended on professional photography.

"As you can see, the inherent physical characteristics of daguerreotypes present several challenges," Arabella continued. "For one, they are incredibly reflective. Depending on the lighting and viewing angle, handholding a dag may provide a clear image of the subject, though you might just as easily be staring back at yourself. And while the glass is protective, it also adds another layer of reflection. In order to photograph dags with any degree of success, it's imperative to control the lighting, which means blocking out anything that could potentially cause a reflection. Hence the black box with a hole for the camera lens."

"A very clever contraption," Faye said.

"Arabella's always been clever," Levon said, still hovering in the doorway.

"I'd like to say the setup is my invention, but I found a version of this setup online and tweaked it," Arabella said, blushing at the compliment. "And now, Levon, don't you think you should go back to your own tasks?"

Levon gave her a mock salute before sauntering away, a gesture that made Faye laugh out loud.

"Honestly, you two are better than a Hallmark movie," she said as her phoned dinged. She glanced at the screen. "It's a text from Bob Wilkes. There's a bully offer coming in on the property. Excuse me, will you? I have some calls to make." She locked down at her jeans and t-shirt. "I'll also need to change into something more business-like."

Arabella knew what a bully offer was; she'd read enough about them in the Toronto papers, buyers bidding on houses before the sellers' official presentation date. She was also sure that it spelled bad news for Luke and Emily, because she had no doubt that *Pemberton on Property* and its executive producer were behind this latest move.

She watched as Faye went outside, all the while thinking of the best way to inform her friend about what was about to go down. Would Emily answer the phone if there were customers in the shop? The answer was almost certainly no. It was the one thing they both agreed on, that the customer in front of you should never be ignored for the one who wasn't. But would she risk a quick glance at her texts? Probably. Arabella had her answer. She just hoped Emily read the message before it was too late.

12

<hr>

EMILY HAD BEEN BACK in the Glass Dolphin for about an hour, the encounter with Miles Pemberton alternately embarrassing and infuriating, the cold making her feel foggy-headed, feverish, and—she could admit it—more than a little bit sorry for herself. Despite her earlier determination to work her shift, she was one sniffle and two sneezes away from calling Caitie to cover for her. And then Poppy Spencer barged into the store, the door slamming shut behind her.

"I'm almost certain that Bob Wilkes is putting together some sort of side deal with Mulacki," Poppy said, her gray eyes flashing with anger.

"A side deal? How is that even possible?" Emily asked, suppressing a sniffle. "Aren't there rules about that?"

"Of course there are, not that Wilkes has ever sweated the small stuff. I was doing some digging on Mulacki's past real estate transactions, trying to determine if there was some pattern to the way he operated. Did his clients typically pay ten percent over asking, that sort of thing. Well, I found a pattern. In almost every single instance where Jay Mulacki & Associates was the listing brokerage, the broker representing the winning buyer was Bob Wilkes."

The way Emily saw it, this time the roles were reversed, with Bob Wilkes Realty as the listing broker and Jay Mulacki representing the buyer. What did it matter how often Wilkes had been successful in the past? Perhaps the head cold was making her cranky, but the last thing she needed was Poppy going on a witch-hunt because of her hatred of Wilkes. Ethically, he might not be able to steer the sellers away from her and Luke's bid, but Emily wasn't willing to take that risk.

"I expect it's just a coincidence."

"And I might be able to accept that, despite being jaded by a dozen years in real estate, except that you'd expect the majority of Bob's clients to be buying property within the tri-community area, not in Toronto, am I right?"

Emily had to concede she was. Even so, she still believed Poppy was overreacting.

"I know what you're thinking, that it doesn't matter if Wilkes won bids in Toronto, but I was once his partner, and I know what he's capable of doing. And let me tell you, that clause in the listing that 'All offers must be sent to and presented by the listing agent' concerns me."

"Isn't that fairly common when expecting multiple offers?"

"It's not uncommon," Poppy admitted reluctantly.

"Then I'm not sure what the problem is. Surely this isn't the first time you've run into a multiple offers situation with Wilkes."

"It's not, but it *is* the first time that Jay Mulacki has been part of the equation, and that brings us back full circle. True, Wilkes's winning record on Mulacki's listings may be luck or coincidence. They may even involve skillful negotiation. But past experience tells me otherwise."

For the first time in this exchange, Emily wondered if Poppy was actually onto something. "Past experience?"

Poppy sighed. "I probably shouldn't be telling you this, but when we were partners, I caught Bob reading offers faxed to our office."

"And that means?"

"That he was reading offers from buyers he didn't represent…at the same time he was trying to bring in an offer of his own. Now to be fair, he did swear up, down, and sideways that he would never disclose the details of the other offers with one of our clients." Poppy held up her hand before Emily could interject. "That said, there were a handful of occasions where his deal was just that little bit sweeter than anyone else's, and I wondered how he'd managed to pull it off at the eleventh hour. A few dollars more, a more attractive closing date, an ever-so-slightly larger deposit, forgoing a home inspection…it could have been luck or good instincts, but I stopped trusting him."

Emily understood how much trust meant to a partnership. Despite their differences, it was the glue that held her and Arabella together.

"It wasn't just because of the trust issue," Poppy continued. "Not many people know this, but when you hire a realtor, you are actually hiring their brokerage. So my reputation was also at stake. I wasn't willing to have that compromised, and I told Bob as much. Suffice it to say, he didn't take it well."

Emily suppressed a grin. Poppy was a top-notch realtor, but tact was not her strong suit. She could only imagine how that conversation went. Still, it sounded as if Bob Wilkes might have a track record of not being completely above board and that was worrisome. Then again, faxes seemed incredibly old-fashioned.

"Do realtors still use faxes?"

"This was a few years back, and in a perfect world, all offers would be presented in sealed envelopes. The reality is that back then offers were often faxed, and today they are usually emailed. In my opinion this is where the character of the listing agent is critical. With inside information and a motivated buyer of their own, he or she can easily coach their buyer to bring the best offer. This is one reason why the listing agent must disclose, in writing and to all interested parties, if they are also representing a buyer in a competition."

"But you'll be at the table on offer night, right? So whatever advantage Wilkes has will be short-lived. I've been reading up on multiple offers. In most cases, especially if the bidding is close, agents are sent back to improve their offers."

"Unfortunately, Wilkes is insisting that all offers are presented without the other agents at the table."

"Can he do that?"

"Yes, if that is how his client has instructed him to proceed."

Emily's phone pinged and she swiped the screen, a frown darkening her face.

"Is something wrong?" Poppy asked.

"It's a text from Arabella. She's at the Hadley house doing an appraisal with Levon. Faye Everett was with her, got a text, and left in a hurry. There's going to be a bully offer on the Hadley house." Emily didn't know exactly what that meant, but it didn't sound good.

"The official term is pre-emptive offer," Poppy said, her frown every bit as dark and deep as her client's. "They usually expire before the delayed offer presentation in an effort to avoid, or 'pre-empt' the established offer process. The seller has the option of seeing the bully offer immediately or holding off until offer day. Did Arabella say who was presenting the offer?"

Emily shook her head. "She doesn't know. Faye left as soon as she got the text from Wilkes."

Poppy's thumbs worked overtime as she tried to connect with Wilkes. She set her phone down after a few minutes, her expression dour.

"Just received confirmation. It's true."

"At least Wilkes let you know," Emily said, trying, despite the odds, to remain hopeful. "That has to mean something."

"Trust me, he wouldn't have if I hadn't called him on it. Slimeball. As a realtor, he is supposed to notify anyone who has expressed an interest in the property of any change to the offer process. An expression of interest includes parties that have booked viewing appointments and viewed the property. That's you and Luke, though I'm actually surprised he answered my text."

"Do we know who the bully offer is from?"

Poppy shook her head. "No. My gut tells me it's Jay Mulacki for

Miles Pemberton, but it could be anyone. I'm not the listing agent, therefore I'm not privy to how many viewings were on the house."

"But you think Mulacki and Wilkes are in cahoots," Emily said, dejection setting in. Had her run-in with Pemberton at the dollar store instigated his bully offer?

"Suspecting they're in cahoots and knowing it are two different things," Poppy said, texting away. "What I need to find out is whether the sellers are willing to look at pre-emptive offers, or if they intend to wait until the original presentation date. Wilkes conveniently left out that detail. I've asked for more information."

Emily's spirits brightened ever so slightly. "Do you mean…can we go in with our own bully offer? Is that allowed?"

"It is but…" Poppy's phone pinged and she glanced at the message, her frown deepening. "The offer is going to be presented today at two p.m."

"Two p.m.? But that's only a couple of hours from now. It's not nearly enough time to…we thought we had five days, not five minutes." Tears streamed down Emily's face. It was all so unfair.

Stupid horoscope.

13

ARABELLA WAS CONCERNED ABOUT EMILY, but she'd been hired to do a job. The next fifteen minutes found her absorbed in taking photographs of the daguerreotype. Once the photos were downloaded to her desktop, she'd be able to zoom in to determine the title of the book the young woman was reading. From there, she could search for it on websites that offered antiquarian books. These details helped bring an object to life, and Arabella prided herself on her ability to do just that.

Satisfied she'd captured the image, she packed up her gear, wandered into the living room, and found Levon lying headfirst underneath the kneehole of the roll-top desk. He pushed himself out and up, a pair of tweezers in one hand, a small LED flashlight in the other, and favored her with his signature lopsided smile. Arabella wondered when—or if—that smile would stop making her feel like a high school kid with a bad crush. The thought infuriated and embarrassed her in equal measure, making her next statement sound more like an accusation than a question.

"I gather you haven't found the key?"

"Ye of little faith," Levon said, brandishing a small brass key. "I found it stuffed inside the seashell drawer pull, middle drawer, left side. It had been rolled into blue adhesive putty, flattened out, and crammed right up to the narrow opening at the top. No way you'd feel it if you tried to tug the drawer open, your fingers wouldn't go up that far. I don't even think I would have discovered it without determination and a decent flashlight. I needed tweezers to remove it. Quite inventive of me, actually."

Arabella had to admit tweezers were inventive. She'd never really considered them for anything but plucking eyebrows. Not that she'd admit as much to Levon.

"Quite. Now, open the desk, already."

Levon inserted the key into the desk's lock and slowly slid the roll-top back to reveal the interior: two rows of eight drawers, four to a side, a small cubbyhole, two center slots for correspondence, and four generously-proportioned bottom drawers. The desktop was solid, careful inspection revealed indentations in the surface made by pens of the past. A circular ink stain in the right-hand corner where an inkpot would have stood added charm. A small key tucked inside the cubbyhole opened the lock on the bottom bank of drawers.

"Gorgeous, isn't it?" he said, opening drawers at random. "Hey, how cool is this?" He carefully removed a parchment document, yellowed by age, and handed it to Arabella.

A. Cutler & Son, Buffalo, New York. Number 073-SD, oak desk, $38. Sold February 19, 1900 to T. Eaton & Co., Toronto, Canada.

"It's amazing that it's stayed with the desk all this time." She looked up to find Levon studying the dovetail of one of the drawers.

"Machine-made, not that I expected anything different given the date of sale," he said, "but beautiful workmanship nonetheless. That said, in today's market it won't fetch nearly what it should, despite the original bill of sale, even if I can find this particular model in an old T. Eaton catalogue. Faye will probably be disappointed to learn that."

"If you'd like, I could write up a history of the company to include with your appraisal." Arabella blushed. "Never mind. I'm sure you were already planning to do that."

Levon grinned. "I was, but you're so much better at it than I am.

Besides, we're in this together. Reminds me a bit about the old days when we were just starting out."

It reminded Arabella of the old days, too, another thing she wasn't about to admit.

"I'll write something up on Cutler Desk and get it to you later this week," she said, her voice all business. "Now, let's check out the rest of the desk."

They opened every drawer without success. "I don't understand it," Arabella said. "Why would Harriet hide the key if all the desk contained was the original bill of sale? It doesn't make sense."

"No, it doesn't," Levon said, "which means we missed something."

Arabella's eyebrows shot up. "Like a secret drawer?"

"Exactly like a secret drawer. Let's remove the drawers again, only this time we'll line them up side-by-side to see if the lengths match up."

"I'm game."

It didn't take long to determine that the right bottom bank of drawers were two inches shorter than the rest. Levon knelt down and smiled. "Voila," he said, pulling out a narrow wooden box from the back of the desk. "I didn't know that Cutler offered this feature."

"The secret drawer could be a special order," Arabella said. "Probably what the 'SD' after the desk number stands for. Is anything inside?"

"There is indeed," Levon said, and passed her a thin document with a blue cardboard cover, the words Joseph R. Fiorini, Barrister & Solicitor, Lount's Landing, Ontario, stamped in black in the bottom left-hand corner. "My guess is it's a copy of Esther Harriet Hadley's will. I'll let you do the honors."

Arabella opened the folder and frowned. "You're half right. It *is* a will, but it's not Esther's." She held out the document so Levon could read the name.

Alexander Murdoch Gilroy.

The name was familiar to Arabella, because a brass plaque on the front of the Sunrise Café proclaimed that the building had once been the establishment of Murdoch Gilroy, Esquire. She'd always assumed Murdoch was Graham's grandfather, though she'd never thought to question it.

But this was *Alexander Murdoch Gilroy.* Was he Graham's father? Another relative?

"Alex was Graham's dad," Levon said, reading her thoughts. "He was killed in a boating accident on Lake Miakoda, six months after his wife, Rose, died of cancer. That was a couple of years before Graham took his plunge into the Dutch River. But why is his will hidden inside this desk?" He went to turn the page when Arabella stopped him.

"Wait. Is it an invasion of privacy if we read it?"

"I don't see how. The man's long dead and buried, and so is Esther. And technically it's part of the estate we've been hired to appraise."

Arabella considered that and saw the logic. But something continued to niggle at her, that sixth sense she got, as if someone was trying to warn her. She'd ignored it when she'd agreed to do the appraisal before consulting Emily. She wasn't about to ignore it again.

"In that case, do you think we could finish off the rest of the appraisal first, and read this somewhere more private?"

"More private? The kitchen table isn't private enough?" Levon's eyes narrowed. "You're worried that Faye will come back and we'll have to show it to her. But we'll have to do that eventually, won't we? Unless you think there's something in here that might impact the current sale of the house. Something that might need us to consult a lawyer."

"That's exactly what I'm thinking."

"In that case, let's do the appraisal and go back to my place. You've got that nosy neighbor and the store will still be open."

She thought back to the last time she'd been at Levon's house, how she'd wound up in his bed after too many snifters of cognac.

Levon grinned. "I promise, strictly business, no cognac."

"No cognac," Arabella repeated, and didn't know whether she felt relieved or disappointed.

14

Emily paced the shop floor, waiting for word from Poppy, sneezing, sniffling, and seething with anger. The realtor had left an hour earlier with assurances that she'd do her best to find out whatever she could, not that she'd sounded overly optimistic.

Neither had Luke, who had been infuriatingly pragmatic. As far as her fiancé was concerned, there would be other houses, and if this one didn't work out, another one would. He'd even said it might be for the best, knowing the amount of work the Hadley house needed. Emily wished she had called him on the store's landline instead of her mobile. At least then she would have had the satisfaction of slamming the receiver. Sometimes technology let you down.

Emily barely heard the doorbell announcing a customer. She looked up to see the smiling face of Sydney Van Fraassen, owner of the recently-opened Sydney's Smoothie Bar. Emily had been inside only once, with the sole objective of welcoming Sydney to Main Street. Upon learning that Emily was a co-owner of the Glass Dolphin, Sydney had jokingly referred to Arabella and Levon as her "furniture parents." They'd given her a gently used sofa bed and chair while she was studying business administration. But none of that explained what Sydney was doing here now, carrying a large, clear beverage container filled with a concoction bluer than the young woman's eyes.

"Word on the street is you lost it today at Dollars to Donuts," Sydney said, flicking a strand of long brown hair away from her face with a toss of her head. "I thought you could use a pick-me-up."

Emily blanched. "Don't tell me…*Outside the Landing?*"

Sydney laughed, her eyes crinkling at the corners. "One and the same. I'll spare you the details. Let's just say Truth Seeker was less than kind in her portrayal of your role in the incident. If I were a betting girl, I'd say Miles Pemberton was her source. You ask me, she's smitten with him. Or at least his celebrity status, such as it is."

Miles Pemberton. That man was becoming the bane of her existence. "I'd tell you my side but, to be honest, it wasn't my finest hour."

"A bad cold can bring the cranky out in the best of us," Sydney said, her face a sympathetic mask. "That's why I brought you a Blue Suede Shoes."

Emily looked down at Sydney's feet. White sneakers. "Blue suede shoes?"

Sydney nodded. "It's my most popular smoothie. Banana, light coconut milk, wild blueberries, and a scoop of all-natural peanut butter. Elvis would be proud. But it's also chock full of nutrients to help you fight a cold or flu. Bananas are rich in vitamin C. Coconut has antiviral and antibacterial properties. Blueberries have an antihistamine effect. And peanut butter contains zinc, which plays an important role in the proper functioning of the immune system in the body."

And here I thought all she did was toss berries into a blender, Emily thought with a flash of guilt. "It sounds like just the ticket, thank you. And thanks for the warning about *Outside the Landing*. At least I'll be prepared."

"No thanks required. Just do me one favor, if you can."

"Name it."

"Find a way to beat Miles Pemberton at his own game."

Sydney was out the door before Emily could ask why. She took a sip of her Blue Suede Shoes, contemplating the possibilities. Only one thing was certain. Hand delivering the smoothie, delicious as it was, had nothing to do with Emily's cold.

And everything to do with Miles Pemberton.

15

———————

Maybe it was psychosomatic, but Sydney's Blue Suede Shoes smoothie had made Emily feel marginally better. She wondered how long that sense of well-being would last once she read the latest missive on *Outside the Landing*, knowing she'd have to face it sooner or later. Might as well be sooner.

The headline said it all. Local Antiques Shop Co-Owner Throws a Hissy Fit. Emily bit her lip and began reading.

Is house hunting with her fiancé making one antiques shop co-owner seriously cranky? Emily Garland was spotted throwing a serious hissy fit at Dollars to Donuts this morning, with none other than Miles Pemberton being the recipient of her diatribe.

Rumor has it that, like Pemberton, Garland is also interested in the old Hadley house and won't go down without a fight, but no one expected this real estate war to end up in fisticuffs.

A word of advice, Ms. Garland. Save yourself some time and heartache and get over it. This reporter has it on good faith that it's a fight you're not going to win.

Emily cursed silently under her breath. *Fisticuffs? Really?* There had been no physical contact. She was a pacifist. A vegetarian. But that wasn't the thing that really upset her. It was that one sentence, the one almost verbatim to what Pemberton had said to Poppy. *Save yourself some time and heartache and get over it.*

Which meant her earlier suspicions were true. Miles Pemberton was Truth Seeker's source, and almost certainly the bully behind the bully offer being presented on the Hadley house.

And there wasn't a darn thing she could do about it.

❧

AT LOOSE ENDS waiting to hear from Poppy, resigned to staying at the Glass Dolphin until closing time, and in no mood to work on advertising and promotion, Emily decided to track down what connection Sydney Van Fraassen might have to Miles Pemberton. She entered Sydney's name into her search engine and was rewarded with an online exclusive article for *Inside the Landing*, posted four months prior.

A HEALTHY ALTERNATIVE

By Kerri St. Amour

Folks looking for a healthy alternative to fast food need look no further than the newly-opened Sydney's Smoothie Bar. Sydney Van Fraassen, 29, was born and raised in Lount's Landing, and is an honors graduate of Brock University. She recently left the fast-paced world of downtown Toronto, where she was a freelance researcher for a number of home-improvement programs on the CKHTV network.

When asked why she opened a smoothie bar in Lount's Landing, Van Fraassen replied, "Toronto is a great city, but I'm a small town girl at heart. Working in television may sound glamorous, but the reality is very different, or at least, my reality was very different. I've been looking for the right opportunity to move back home for some time."

Van Fraassen uses a variety of fresh and frozen fruits and vegetables, supplemented with frozen yogurt, whey protein, and organic ingredients like coconut and almond milk, green tea, honey, and natural peanut butter. Her celebrity-and-movie-themed blends, such as the Wizard of Oz-*inspired Ruby*

Slippers (beets, strawberries, mangos, apples, carrots, and whey protein powder), are as good for you as they are good.

Find Sydney's Smoothie Bar at 110 Main Street and tell Sydney you read about her in Inside the Landing *to save 15% on your first order.*

How did Sydney go from being a freelance researcher to running a smoothie bar? Emily smiled: maybe about the way she'd gone from being a journalist to co-owner of an antiques store.

Interesting, though, that Sydney had worked as a freelance researcher for home improvement shows. Had she worked for Pemberton? Emily knew from personal experience that freelance meant you never knew where your next assignment was coming from. Not an easy life, though you could eke out a decent living if you developed a good reputation.

A good reputation. Ruin that and you could plunge from freelance favorite to pathetic pariah. That had to be it.

Emily went to CKHTV's website next, clicking on the tab titled "Shows," found *Pemberton on Property*, scanned the program credits for Sydney's name and found it.

Emily sat back. What exactly had Miles Pemberton done to make Sydney Van Fraassen leave CKHTV? Was the fact that they were both in the Landing pre-planned or coincidence?

She wasn't sure, though she knew Arabella didn't believe in coincidences. And Arabella was seldom wrong. Emily couldn't wait to find out what her partner knew about her "furniture child's" past.

16

Arabella drove up Levon's driveway, once again admiring the slate blue board-and-batten façade with carefully painted cream trim. The house was on an acre of land, with a stream running along the west side of the property, and a row of trees acting as a natural fence along the east. A large wooden barn, painted rustic red, stored his antique finds and provided a spot to restore and refinish the furniture when warranted.

"Sometimes you have to leave the age in, and sometimes," Levon had told her, his words befitting a person with years of experience and a practiced eye, "the only way to sell a piece is to make it pretty again."

For a brief moment, Arabella could almost imagine herself coming home on a warm midsummer's evening after a long shift at the Glass Dolphin, Levon waiting for her on the front porch, his arms ready to scoop her up into a massive hug. They'd sit on the wicker rockers, stored inside now that winter was setting in, and they'd swap stories about their respective days, laughing, her head resting on his shoulder as the day's trials and tribulations melted from her mind. She shook her head, willing the image away.

That was then. This was now.

WITH THE EXCEPTION of stainless steel appliances in the kitchen, everything in Levon's house appeared to be antique or vintage, from the framed maps of nineteenth-century Toronto and Cedar County on the sage-green walls, to the leather-upholstered Arts & Crafts chairs, lamps, and area rug in the living room. The overall impression was one of tasteful masculinity. If Levon was dating, Arabella thought, the woman in his life hadn't yet made her mark. Not that it mattered, she reminded herself. Her ex-husband's love life was of no concern to her.

She took a seat across from Levon at the round mission oak dining room table, anxious to begin reading the will. The appraisal of the contents at the Hadley house was taking longer than she'd anticipated, and Levon hadn't even started cataloguing the books inside the stacking bookcase. It was just like him to save what he'd consider the best for last. Rare and antiquarian books, Arabella knew, were one of her ex-husband's passions.

"Ready to get started?" Levon asked.

Arabella nodded and turned back the pale blue cardboard, making sure that Levon could read along with her.

THE LAST WILL AND TESTAMENT OF ALEXANDER MURDOCH GILROY. Prepared by Joseph R. Fiorini, Barrister & Solicitor, 630 Main Street, Lount's Landing, ON, 555-853-6464.

"I've never heard of Joseph Fiorini, but you've lived here a lot longer than I have," Arabella said. "Does the name or location ring any bells?"

"He used to have a general practice, wills, real estate, not the sort of lawyer I'd expect Alexander Gilroy to hire. He had a firm of corporate lawyers in Toronto to do his bidding. But maybe he wanted to support local business."

Or maybe, Arabella thought, *he didn't want his corporate law firm to know about this will.* "Where is Joseph Fiorini now?"

"Last I heard, Fiorini was splitting his time between Florida in the winter and Muskoka in the summer, but that could have changed. Were you thinking of contacting him? Because I'm pretty sure solicitor-client privilege would still apply, even though Alexander is deceased. And we're getting ahead of ourselves. We haven't even read the will."

"I only asked if you'd heard of him," Arabella said, though the idea of contacting Fiorini *had* crossed her mind. She turned the page and skimmed the usual legalese of revoking other wills and codicils until she reached the appointment of the executor. Stanford McLelland. The owner of McLelland Insurance Brokerage *and* her former employer. Even so, she'd never heard him mention Alexander, even when they'd discussed Graham's death.

"Did you know Alexander was friends with Stanford McLelland?"

Levon shook his head. "No, he's a good fifteen years older than me, and Graham and I really didn't hang out. Anyway, just because Stanford's the executor doesn't mean that he and Alexander were best friends. He might have picked him because he could be trusted."

"But he still would have told Stanford, right?" Arabella said. "I mean, you don't just make someone an executor without consulting them first, do you?"

Levon shrugged. "I don't know, maybe you do. You could always ask him."

Arabella planned to do just that. She'd left the insurance brokerage to open the Glass Dolphin, a move Stanford had encouraged. They remained on good terms, occasionally having a glass of wine and sharing a plate of Full Noose Nachos at The Hanged Man's Noose. If there was anything to discover about Alexander Gilroy's will, she was sure that Stanford would tell her.

She turned to the last page and gave an involuntary gasp. Arabella read the words over and over again, until they were a blur.

I hereby bequeath the property and contents of 21 Walnut Street, Lount's Landing, Ontario, to the love of my life, Esther Harriet Hadley, as a life interest, for her own use absolutely. Upon her death, ownership of the house and all contents will transfer to my son, Graham Alexander Gilroy. My remaining properties and assets, once liquidated, shall be split as follows: 25 percent to Esther Harriet Hadley, 25 percent to Kids Come First, Charitable

Registration No. ON-5557676333, and 50 percent to my son, Graham Alexander Gilroy.

Levon shifted back in his chair, a stunned look on his face. "Whoa. That goes a long way to explaining why we found this will in Esther's desk. But you have to wonder how this never came to light before now."

"There's a lot more than that to wonder about," Arabella said. "Why did their relationship end if Esther truly was the love of Alexander's life? And what about his wife? She couldn't have appreciated being second choice."

"Maybe Rose never knew about Esther. Maybe she didn't care. Either way, I don't see how it matters. As for the relationship between Alex and Esther ending, sometimes those decisions are out of our control." He gave Arabella a sad smile. "I speak from experience."

Arabella flushed, knowing she'd walked right into that one. To this day, Levon insisted he hadn't cheated on her with Camilla. Sometimes she almost believed him. "Right, well, whatever," she said, more brusquely than she intended. "What's our next step?"

"Do we even need a next step? We were hired to appraise the contents of the house, not to dig into Esther's past."

"What about the will? Do we give it to Faye or put it back where we found it?"

"I'm inclined to put it back where we found it, if only to protect Esther's secret, but the right thing to do is give it to Faye Everett. It could have an impact on the estate."

"What sort of impact?"

"The sort of impact that is none of our business." Levon studied her. "You *are* going to drop this, aren't you? Because I never trust it when you acquiesce so easily."

"Of course I'm going to drop this," Arabella said, her fingers crossed under the table. *Just as soon as I find out why that will was hidden and what, if anything, it means to the estate.* And her first call was going to be to Stanford McLelland.

17

ARABELLA REFUSED Levon's offer to stay for supper and took the will with her, promising to hand-deliver it to Faye the next time they met. No need to tell Levon she planned to ask Stanford to join her for dinner tonight at the Noose.

Not only did Stanford forgive the short notice, he sounded ridiculously pleased to hear from her, a reminder to Arabella that she had to make more of an effort to keep in touch. They arranged to meet at seven, and by the time Arabella got there, Alexander Murdoch Gilroy's will in her handbag, he was already seated at a table near the rear of the pub, a frosted mug of beer in front of him.

"It's been too long," he said, as she slid into the seat across from him. "But it occurred to me, after you hung up, that this probably isn't just dinner. What's up? I haven't heard of any new murders, thankfully. Does this have anything to do with Emily and Luke wanting to buy the old Hadley house? I read about Emily's run in with Miles Pemberton in Dollars to Donuts."

Emily had a run in with Miles Pemberton? When did that happen? She was supposed to be covering the store all day. Arabella must have looked confused because Stanford clarified.

"You can read all about it in *Outside the Landing,* though

considering the source, I expect the coverage was skewed against Emily. I'm sure she'll tell you the real story when you see her."

Arabella sighed. "I'm sure she will, but it's not like we can post her side of the story. We've both learned from past experience that folks follow that horrible blog and trust it as if it were the gospel truth. And here I thought we were beyond being tarred and feathered by that woman."

Stanford took Arabella's hand. "I think you're overreacting. The Glass Dolphin is a well-regarded business on Main Street and everyone likes Emily. Besides, she's not a hothead."

"Unlike me," Arabella said with a smile. She waved down Stanford's attempt to object. "Oh, it's no secret that I can be a bit of a hothead. I might even take a misguided sense of pride in it. Anyway, let's order so I can get to the reason I called you."

✒

THEY BOTH ORDERED the house special, a steak sandwich with a side of onion rings, and Arabella savored every medium rare bite. Honestly, vegetarians had no idea what they were missing. She wiped her mouth, then took a sip from her house red. It was time to get to the point.

"Levon and I were hired to appraise the contents of the Hadley house. Well, actually, I was hired to appraise a daguerreotype on Levon's recommendation…and to assist Levon with the appraisal, if it was deemed necessary."

Stanford grinned. "Something tells me Levon deemed it was necessary."

Arabella blushed. She had been working for Stanford when she'd married Levon, had cried on his shoulder when she'd suspected Levon of cheating. Come to think of it, he'd never believed it. *Men, they always stuck together.* "It's always good to have a second opinion."

The grin broadened. "Is that why you invited me to dinner? To get my opinion? Or is there something more clandestine going on?"

"Nothing so cloak-and-dagger," Arabella said, and filled him in on the locked roll-top desk, the hidden key, and the secret compartment.

"Levon's sleuthing skills are almost as impressive as yours. But I'm not sure where I fit in."

Arabella reached into her handbag, pulled out the will, and set it on the table. "We found this document inside the secret compartment. It's the last will and testament of Alexander Murdoch Gilroy. It splits the estate between Graham Gilroy and Esther Harriet Hadley. You're listed as the executor."

"I recognize the cover, and the name of the lawyer," Stanford said. "There's only one problem."

"What's that?"

"To the best of my knowledge, this isn't his last will and testament."

18

———

ARABELLA STARED AT STANFORD, trying to process what he'd just told her.

"There were three wills," Stanford said. "One before this one, and one after. Unfortunately, I don't know where the one after resides, the terms, or when it was signed. Alex had become increasingly secretive, almost to the point of being neurotic. Then, less than a week before his death, Alex informed me that I was 'off the hook' as his executor." He smiled, though there was no warmth in the expression. "I suppose you want me to tell you what I know."

"I would."

"Then with your consent, I'd like to take it from the beginning."

Arabella would have liked to cut to the end, but she also knew that, like the antiques she sold, the smallest detail could make a difference. It occurred to her that she might also be placing her ex-employer in a difficult situation. "I'd appreciate that. If you're able to."

"To be honest, it would be a relief to talk about it after all these years. Some secrets weigh heavily on your soul."

In Arabella's experience, all secrets tended to weigh heavily, with enough time and perspective. "I'm listening."

Stanford took a deep breath, then began. "Alex and I met in the ninth grade. My father had started the insurance brokerage a few years earlier, he was respected in the community, and financially our family was doing better than most. But there was no comparison between dad's modest success and the Gilroys' wealth. His parents were old money, so old you didn't question where it might have come from, though rumor has it Murdoch Gilroy had done well by prohibition in Canada. You'd think having nosebleed money would have made Alex popular, but the reverse was true. Back then, Miakoda Falls was the town the mill built, and Lount's Landing was no more than a hamlet.

"Alex was painfully shy and sort of nerdy, with super-short hair and wire-rimmed glasses, and his mother ironed a crease into his blue jeans. On top of that, he was probably the second-worst athlete anyone at the school had ever seen. Ducked when a baseball came his way, couldn't make a basket if he stood on a ladder, and never got the hang of skating backwards, let alone learn how to stickhandle a hockey puck."

"The second-worst athlete. Were you…?"

"The worst? Yup. So there we were, two misfits trying to make it to graduation without getting bullied or beaten up, and we clicked. We were inseparable, or were until…but I don't want to speak ill of the dead."

Arabella wondered if he was referring to Esther Hadley or Camilla, though if she were a betting person, she'd bet on Camilla. She shifted in her seat.

"But back to Esther," Stanford continued, and Arabella's suspicions about Camilla were confirmed. "We first met her at a pub in Lakeside. Alex and I were recent University of Toronto grads, celebrating our last blast of freedom before entering the workforce—me at my father's insurance brokerage with the view to taking it over someday, and Alex as the manager of the Gilroy family's considerable real estate holdings." He grimaced. "At least, they were considerable until Graham took over."

Was that why Alex's estate was split fifty-fifty? Arabella wondered. *Because he knew his son would blow through his inheritance?*

"You're probably wondering if Graham's financial ineptitude factors into any of this," Stanford said, as if reading her mind. "The answer is yes, though not in the way you might expect. But first let me tell you about Alex and Esther."

His eyes took on a faraway look. "Alex had become a bit of a player in university, the family money finally working for him. All that changed the night we met Esther. Alex fell for her hard and fast, not that anyone could blame him. One look at Esther Hadley and you could tell that she was special, not just because she was breathtakingly beautiful, but because she had this air about her, as if no one would ever be good enough for her. Unfortunately, she had lowered her standards long enough to marry Martin Hadley, a smooth-talking con artist who'd never worked an honest day in his life. Not that Alex had any intention of allowing Martin to stay in the picture."

"How did he expect to accomplish that?"

"Not just he," Stanford said. "They. It wasn't long before Esther fell every bit as hard for Alex. At least that's what she led him to believe. That's when the real trouble began."

19

———

If Arabella's interest had been piqued upon finding the will, it was on steroids now. "What sort of trouble?"

"Alex and Esther started seeing each other and not just for coffee, if you take my meaning," Stanford said, a faint flush spreading across his cheeks. "They were cautious at first, but as the days turned into weeks, they became careless. Their affair was the worst kept secret in Lount's Landing, though Martin seemed oblivious."

"Surely no one's that dense."

"Martin was a con artist. He wanted a piece of the Gilroy money. And Esther was his way to get it."

"But if Esther left him for Alex—"

"Is that what you think?" Stanford shook his head. "Esther might have led Alex to believe that she wanted to leave Martin, but it was never going to happen."

Arabella frowned. "Then why not end the affair?"

"Because it was all part of her master plan. Martin and Esther were like Bonnie and Clyde—without banks and machine guns, but robbers just the same. Unfortunately, Alex didn't see it. When I tried to warn him, he accused me of being jealous. Not long after, Alex purchased the Walnut Street house, and he hired Esther to decorate it."

"So she's the one to blame for all the floral wallpaper."

"Yep, cabbage roses and ivy. Then he asked Esther to move in, naively believing that she would file for divorce, or at the very least, legal separation. The last thing Alex expected was Martin to take up residence, but that's exactly what happened."

"That's bold. But wouldn't that make Alex see the light?"

"You'd think so, but Esther claimed that she was worried about Martin's mental health, that they were sleeping in separate bedrooms, that it was just a temporary arrangement until Martin found a full-time job. A less infatuated man might have seen the con for what it was and walked away. Not Alex. He stayed around for whatever crumbs Esther was willing to toss him, convinced that the only thing holding them back was Martin. Get him out of the picture and…" Stanford let the sentence dangle.

"And he and Esther would live happily ever after?"

"Eventually, even Alex knew it was a fairy tale. Or at least that's what I believed at the time. Later on, I wasn't as sure."

"Why not?"

Stanford stared down at his hands, deliberating, then said, "A few weeks later, Martin was killed in a single vehicle crash in Miakoda Falls. His blood alcohol level was twice the legal limit, but that's not what caused the accident. At least, it wasn't the only cause."

"If not that, what?"

"Someone tampered with his brakes while he was inside the bar being over-served. Witnesses saw him in the parking lot behind the bar, arguing with another man, a man in a faded jean jacket who fit Alex's general description. Except Alex had an alibi for that evening. Me."

"Were you with him?"

"For most of the evening. We had dinner together at a restaurant where plenty of people saw us. The thing is, we'd gone our separate ways a good half hour before Martin left the bar, but I was vague on the timing and the police didn't question it. After all, this was Alexander Gilroy, and the Gilroy name had plenty of influence. Besides, everyone knew that Alex wouldn't be caught dead in distressed denim. By then he was a walking advertisement for men's fashion, a real clotheshorse, never stepped a foot outside without being perfectly groomed, suit, tie, crisp white shirt, diamond cufflinks. No more ironed jeans."

"And yet, you still have your doubts. Is that what you meant about secrets weighing heavily on your soul?"

Stanford nodded. "For a long time after that, Alex and I kept our distance. It felt safer that way, for both of us."

"Was anyone ever arrested in Martin's death?"

"No. To the best of my knowledge, it's still an open, if very cold, case, though I doubt the police have given it much thought in years."

"What about Esther?"

"Alex allowed her to stay at the house on Walnut Street. He paid the overhead, along with her basic living expenses, but their love affair ended with Martin's death. Whether that was guilt on Alex's part, a broken heart on the part of Esther's, or a combination of the two is anyone's guess. As time went on, Alex became prone to dark moods and bouts of self-loathing. Esther became increasingly reclusive, and rumors started floating around that the house was haunted, rumors I suspect she perpetuated to keep folks away. A few months after Martin's accident, Alex met Rose at a political fundraiser. She didn't have Esther's looks or charisma, but she could be very persuasive."

"I gather she persuaded Alex," Arabella said with a smile.

"She did indeed, though I always suspected the marriage was one of convenience for both of them, rather than anything passionate. Nonetheless, they were married within weeks of meeting, and Graham came along a year later. As a power couple, they were well suited, and the Gilroy portfolio of properties continued to expand. But money doesn't mean a life without challenges, and they certainly had their fair share with Graham.

And then Rose died, and whatever light remained inside Alex died with her."

"And the will?"

"Despite their wealth, like most married couples, the terms of their wills were identical and very straightforward. Should Alex die first, everything would go to Rose, and vice versa. If they died together, or before another will was made, the estate would pass on to Graham." Stanford paused. "Alex changed his will soon after Rose died. He didn't want Graham to get the entire estate, knowing he'd burn through it faster than a forest fire, but he couldn't bring himself to cut him off altogether. He asked me to be the executor."

"And despite the past, or maybe because of it, you said yes," Arabella said.

"I was reluctant at first. Our friendship had been strained since Martin's death, but once Alex told me he wanted to leave the house on Walnut Street and twenty-five percent of his estate to Esther, I agreed. In my mind, con artist or not, she deserved that much. At least she did if Alex killed her husband. Even if he didn't have anything to do with it, he'd been supporting Esther's reclusive lifestyle for so long, she wouldn't have been able to survive without his help. Alex knew that. And in his heart, Esther would always be the love of his life. Romanticized over the years, yes, but who hasn't done that with a relationship long over?"

Was that what she was doing with Levon? Romanticizing a relationship long over? Arabella pushed the thought from her mind.

"Levon told me that Alexander died in a boating accident in Lake Miakoda. I'm not sure if it's important, but can you tell me what happened?"

"His canoe capsized. Alex drowned, despite being a strong swimmer. The toxicology report showed trace amounts of alcohol in his system." Stanford shook his head. "Alex's motto was 'water on the water' and 'beer on the pier.' It wasn't like him to have a couple of drinks and then go paddling. I've always suspected that he committed suicide, what with Rose gone and Esther still grieving the loss of Martin, but his death was ruled accidental."

Arabella was reminded of Graham's death. *Like father, like son?*

How many secrets were buried with both of them, including the possibility of a third will?

The will. She had to stop letting her mind wander. "What I don't understand is why Esther made such an elaborate effort to conceal the will. Why go to all that trouble when it clearly stated she was to inherit a life interest in the house, and twenty-five percent of the estate."

"I'm not convinced it was Esther that hid the will," Stanford said.

"But if not Esther, then who?" But even as she said the words, Arabella knew the answer.

Graham Gilroy. The one who insisted that everything be left in the house, exactly as it was.

Except, as Stanford had pointed out, the will she'd found with Levon wasn't Alex's last will and testament. Had Graham known that? Had Esther? What if they'd both been cut out of the third will? Would Alexander Gilroy have done that? Disinherited his own son, and the supposed love of his life?

She posed the question to Stanford.

"It's possible," he admitted, after lengthy consideration. "Alex could be incredibly generous, but he demanded loyalty above all else. If he thought that loyalty had been compromised…if, for some unknown reason he believed either Graham or Esther had conspired against him in some way…but they both stood to inherit under the terms of the second will. It doesn't make sense."

Neither did finding a will hidden inside a secret compartment. Arabella sipped her wine, considering the possibilities. If this were a movie, there'd be a safe behind one of the many ghastly paintings hanging on the walls. And inside the safe, there'd be a third and final will. But this wasn't a movie, and she doubted that any such safe existed.

But doubt and certainty were two very different things, and it was a loose end that needed to be tied up. Because if Graham *had* been cut out of his father's estate, he couldn't have been the legal owner of 21 Walnut Street at the time of his death. And if he wasn't the legal owner, then Camilla Mortimer-Gilroy couldn't have inherited the property. Which meant Faye Everett and

Megan Sutcliffe were potentially selling something they didn't own.

Damn. She'd have to ask Levon to meet her back at the house. But first, she had to call Faye. She owed her that much, even if it meant breaking Emily's heart.

"I have to go," Arabella said, and tossed some bills on the table. She was out the door before Stanford could ask her why.

20

Arabella called Faye Everett from the parking lot behind the Noose. "I have a matter of some importance to discuss with you, hopefully before you accept the bully offer."

"Well, you're in luck on that count. It was an extremely good offer from Miles Pemberton, but the bank strongly suggested that we wait for Monday, offer day, as originally planned. There's a twenty-four hour irrevocable, so we have time to think it over, though Megan's involvement with Pemberton Productions might pose a conflict of interest. Seems *Outside the Landing* got wind of it somehow."

Arabella was certain the wind beneath that particular sail had blown in courtesy of Faye, but she kept that opinion to herself. The last thing she needed was to get in the middle of a sibling rivalry. "I hadn't heard, but I don't tend to rely on *Outside the Landing* for my news updates."

Faye laughed. "Then you're the only one. Anyway, you said you have a matter of some importance to discuss with me. I take it this has something to do with the appraisal?"

"It might be better to meet in person," Arabella said, ignoring the question. "Preferably at the Hadley house."

"It's almost nine o'clock on a Wednesday night and I'm wiped. Can't this wait until morning?"

"Are you sincere about not reviewing any additional offers until Monday?"

"I am, not that it's any of your concern."

For the first time, Faye sounded annoyed. Arabella ignored that, too. "Then it can wait, but I'll have to arrange for Emily to cover the store. It's her usual day off. How's ten-thirty sound?"

"Like a reasonable hour. Will Levon be coming as well?"

Levon. Arabella really should have called him first. Well, she'd just have to hope he'd come through. "That's the plan."

"In that case, I'll see you both tomorrow morning." Faye hung up before Arabella could say good-bye.

✒

ARABELLA'S first call was to Emily. "I know you're under the weather, but I've got to meet Levon at the Hadley house about the appraisal tomorrow morning and—"

A sniffle, then, "No problem. I'd only be sitting around at home, worried about the Hadley house, and feeling sorry for myself. Besides, Luke's at the Toronto International Snowmobile, ATV & Powersports Show until Sunday. I'll be lucky to hear from him. I may as well do something constructive."

"Thanks," Arabella said, hanging up before Emily could ask any questions. They were close, but, even so, she didn't think it was her place to share what Faye had told her. That was Poppy's job. Now if only it would be as easy with Levon. She took a deep breath and dialed.

He answered on the first ring. "Hey."

"I had dinner with Stanford tonight. At the Noose."

"I thought we agreed not to pursue the will business."

"I didn't agree not to pursue it. I said I'd hand the will over to Faye the next time I saw her. Which I fully intend to do. She's meeting us at the Hadley house tomorrow morning at ten-thirty."

"Us?"

"I assumed you'd be there, since you haven't even started to catalogue the paintings or the books." In truth, she hadn't actually thought of that until just now, but it made sense. Bonus points for quick thinking.

"Nice save, not that I believe it for a moment. Care to fill me in on whatever you and Stan conjured up?"

"There was no conjuring."

"And yet, you've taken it upon yourself to call a meeting." Levon sighed. "I should have known you'd go all Detective Carpenter on me."

Arabella ignored the barb. "Faye is expecting you to be there."

"I'll consider myself summoned."

"Thanks, and Levon…"

"Yes?"

"Can you get there before us, take all paintings down?"

"Take all the paintings down?" Levon sounded confused, then laughed. "Wait a second, are you expecting to find a secret wall safe? Like in the movies?" He was still laughing when Arabella ended the call.

21

———————

ARABELLA ARRIVED a few minutes before ten-thirty on Thursday morning, pleased to see Faye's SUV and Levon's pickup already there. She took a deep breath, knowing what lay ahead of her.

Faye opened the front door as Arabella got out of her car. "Come in, I stopped at the store for some cookies, and I've got the kettle on for tea. Or I can make coffee. There's one of those pod-makers stashed in the cupboard, along with an endless variety of pods, caffeine in all its glory. Levon's taking all the paintings off the walls and documenting them for the record. Apparently it's easier for him do the appraisal in his home office."

Bless Levon for thinking on his feet, Arabella thought, suddenly apprehensive. Should she have told Stanford what she was planning to do? Or maybe she should have consulted a lawyer. Yes, in hindsight she probably should have consulted a lawyer. Well, it was too late now.

"Tea would be lovely."

They settled in at the kitchen table, Levon joining them as Arabella poured the tea and Faye set about getting lemon, milk, and sugar, along with a small plate of digestive cookies. *An appropriate choice*, Arabella thought. What she had to say would be difficult to digest. She was wondering how to start when Faye got to the point.

"So, what's this matter of importance?"

"Levon and I were able to open the desk," Arabella said, and explained how and where they'd found the key.

"Impressive investigative skills aside, I gather the two of you found something."

"We did." Arabella opened her handbag, removed the will, and slid it towards Faye.

Faye's eyebrows shot up. "The Last Will and Testament of Alexander Murdoch Gilroy," she said, flipping to the beneficiary section. "I'm not sure why Esther would have taken such pains to hide it."

"I don't think Esther hid it. I think Graham did, though it's equally possible they were in on it together."

"In on it? You make them sound like co-conspirators in fraud. Why?"

"I know Stanford McLelland, the executor of the will, quite well. He's my former employer, and he's as honest a man as you'll find. Alexander told him that he was 'off the hook' as executor. That was about a week before Alexander's death."

"Meaning he drew up another will," Faye said.

Arabella nodded. "Stanford doesn't know where that will is, or what it contained."

"But you suspect that final will may have disinherited Graham, and possibly Esther as well."

"I realize it's a leap but after talking to Stanford, yes, I think it's possible."

"If that's the case…" Levon said, and stopped mid sentence.

Faye finished for him. "If that's the case, Camilla might not have inherited this house from Graham. You also believe the third and final will is hidden somewhere in the house." She drummed her fingers on the table, studying Arabella with narrowed eyes. "Besides a hearsay conversation from your ex-employer, there is nothing to support your theory of a third will. In fact, it's entirely possible that you've fabricated this entire story to give your friend, Emily, more time to arrange financing. It's also possible that you've leapt to that conclusion because of your dislike for my aunt."

Arabella bristled. "I can assure you that I do not fabricate stories. Furthermore, my feelings for Camilla have nothing to do with this."

"Relax, Arabella. I believe you, much as I'd rather not." Faye sighed. "Part of me wants to ignore this and proceed as planned. After all, we're not accepting offers until Monday. So why is it I can imagine court cases and endless complications? Never mind, don't answer that. I'll call Bob Wilkes and tell him to cancel the open house on Sunday and temporarily take the house off the market."

"Under the circumstances, do you want us to continue with the appraisal?" Levon asked. "After all, the estate is paying our tab."

Arabella glared at Levon. Trust him to try to ruin the opportunity to search for the third will just because he might be out a few bucks. "We're not concerned about getting paid," she said, avoiding Levon's gaze. "We're concerned about the truth."

Faye favored them with a thin-lipped smile. "Thank you, but rest assured, you will be paid, if not by the estate, then by me. What I can't afford is to have this dragging on *ad nauseam*. Make the appraisal your top priority, and while you're at it, search every nook and cranny for that elusive third will. But be forewarned. If, after your best efforts, you come up empty, I'm going to make the assumption that no such will exists, and the house will go back on the market. Are we on the same page?"

Arabella glanced at Levon, nodded unhappily. "We are."

"In that case, I'll leave you to it." Faye stood up, a malicious gleam in her dark eyes. "You know, there is one bright note in all of this."

"What's that?"

"Megan is going to freak out when I tell her."

22

———

BETWEEN ASSISTING THE OCCASIONAL BROWSER, and making one hard-fought sale—a rewired Art Deco torchiere lamp that had been marked down to the point of negligible profit—Emily researched bully offers. She read that RECO, the Real Estate Council of Ontario, wanted to ban the practice. One article said bully offers were considered a controversial practice, further suggesting that sellers who held out for offer day were more likely to benefit from a bidding war. She just hoped the representatives for Camilla's estate felt the same way.

Her mind wandered back to her conversation with Sydney. What did she have against Miles Pemberton? Was it something to do with her research work for *Pemberton on Property*? Or was there a more personal reason?

It had been a very long day, and mercifully it was finally time to close. She flipped the OPEN sign over and turned off all but the emergency lights, more than ready to embrace her mom's favorite cold remedy—hot lemon with a double shot of whisky, followed by a warm bed.

A warm bed. It wouldn't be long before she'd be sharing that bed with Luke every night, the two of them firmly ensconced in the

Hadley house. Except it wouldn't be the Hadley house any longer, it would be the Surmanski house. Emily Garland-Surmanski. It had a nice ring to it. On cue, her cell rang. Poppy Spencer. Emily took a deep breath and answered, expecting the worst, hoping for the best.

"I just had coffee with Bob Wilkes," Poppy said without preamble. "The bully offer on 21 Walnut was not accepted."

"That's good news for us, right?" Emily asked, suddenly unsure. Were they holding out for an insane amount of money? Suddenly the idea of a bidding war scared her as much as the idea of losing the house to Miles Pemberton.

"Good news? Not exactly. The property has been taken off the market. At this point, no offers will be considered, today, tomorrow, or in the foreseeable future."

Off the market was not one of the possible scenarios Emily and Luke had considered. "I don't understand. Why would they do that?"

Poppy sighed. "You'd have to ask your business partner about that."

Arabella? The same Arabella who asked me to cover her shift so she could complete the appraisal? "What does Arabella have to do with this?"

"All I know is what Bob Wilkes told me. During their appraisal of the contents, Levon and Arabella found a document in the Hadley house that requires further investigation. The executors are exercising extreme caution."

"What sort of document?"

"No idea, nor does Bob. At least that's what he told me and I'm inclined to believe him. He really was perplexed—and uncharacteristically apologetic. He didn't appreciate the bully offer any more than we did. In fact, he told me he'd been rooting for you and Luke."

Bob. Not Wilkes. Not Bob Wilkes. Just Bob. There must have been extra cream in that coffee. "Are you sure we can trust him on this, Poppy? Knowing what you do about his past dealings?"

"For all his faults, Bob would never take on a listing knowing there were potential legal problems. No reputable agent would. And he'd never tell me that a house had been taken off the market if it wasn't true. Pulling a stunt like that could cost him his real estate license, or a suspension that would remain part of his permanent record. It wouldn't be worth the risk."

Maybe it was the way she said the words, as if by rote, but Emily was pretty sure Poppy was still holding something back. "What aren't you telling me?"

There was a long pause, so long that Emily wondered if the call had dropped, then, "This is between us, but he's having agent's remorse over getting mixed up with Mulacki and Pemberton. Something happened, though what that something is I honestly don't know."

"But you have a guess."

Another long pause, then, "Reading between the lines? I think Pemberton may have overstepped his authority or his budget, and Mulacki presented the bully offer anyway. But Bob assured me Pemberton and Mulacki had nothing to do with the house being taken off the market. That's on Arabella and Levon finding a document."

"In that case," Emily said, "it's time for me to call Arabella."

❧

EMILY'S PHONE call went straight to Arabella's voice mail. She left a message asking her to call her back ASAP, sent a text to underscore the importance of it, then called Luke, snowmobile show be damned, her emotions alternating between anger and angst as she filled him in. It was bad enough the house had been taken off the market, right? But for Arabella not to have told her…they were business partners. And friends. Or at least they were supposed to be.

Luke was his usual pragmatic self. "Not much we can do but adopt a wait-and-see attitude, my love," he'd said. "I'm sure Arabella had her reasons for not telling you. Maybe it was some sort of legal thing."

Some sort of legal thing. Well maybe it was, and maybe it wasn't. Emily hung up, feeling unsettled, and headed back to her apartment, sniffling all the way.

Back in her own digs, she made herself a hot lemon with honey and a double shot of whiskey, swallowed two aspirin, and flipped open her tablet to read the latest installment from *Outside the Landing.* As a former journalist, it annoyed her that this was how the townsfolk got most of their local news. But she was sucked into the vortex with everyone else, even though she'd recently been a victim to Truth Seeker's gossip-wielding wrath. She was grateful that a new story had replaced her escapade at Dollars to Donuts.

> *No Bullies Allowed!*
>
> *An anonymous source has informed this blogger that a bully offer, registered on the old Hadley house, has been firmly rejected. An open bid process will take place on Monday at 6 p.m. as per the original listing. While my source could not (or is that Would Not?) reveal the name of the bidder, we have since learned that Pemberton on Property's executive producer, Megan Sutcliffe, is a beneficiary of Esther Harriet Hadley's estate. Can you say Conflict of Interest?*

Emily took a sip of her whisky-infused hot lemon, the first genuine smile of the day crossing her face. She didn't know why the Hadley house had been taken off the market, but she knew more than Truth Seeker. And that felt pretty damn good.

23

───────

Arabella watched Faye pull onto Walnut Street, bracing herself for a lecture from Levon.

"You couldn't leave well enough alone, could you?" he asked, pacing the kitchen floor. "What part of 'you're an antiques shop owner, not a detective' don't you understand? Now I'm stuck playing Joe Hardy to your Nancy Drew, instead of finishing what was supposed to be a simple estate appraisal."

"To be fair, we *can* do both," Arabella said. "All this does is add a twist to the tale."

"And don't we know just how much you love to twist your tales."

"What's that supposed to mean?"

"Nothing. Forget it. With any luck, we'll be finished in a few hours. Now get your magnifying glass and put on your deerstalker cap. It's time to get started."

☞

Arabella didn't have a deerstalker, but she had brought a magnifying glass and jeweler's loupe, along with her trusty DSLR camera. She hadn't downloaded the daguerreotype photographs she'd shot yesterday, but there was still plenty of room on the memory card if she needed to take more pictures.

Because Levon had already removed all the paintings from the walls—they hadn't found a secret safe—they decided to start there.

"Anything with a canvas back can be eliminated immediately, so let's put those aside first," Levon said. "That will leave us with anything that's got a paper backing. Those should include notations on the paper, usually who did the framing and when. Occasionally there's a business card glued on, or other documentation to support the authenticity of the artwork or limited edition."

Arabella knew all of that, but if Levon thought he was in charge, things would go a whole lot smoother. "You got it, Joe Hardy."

There were fifteen paintings in all, still lifes of fruit, country landscapes, and summers by the seaside. None revealed anything remotely suspicious. Nor did the half dozen Trisha Romance collector plates housed inside ornate gilt-leaf frames.

"I think we can safely discount the artwork," Levon said, "and not just because we didn't find a will. I know art is in the eye of the beholder, and bless Esther Harriet Hadley if she loved each and every one of these, but we'd be lucky to get a thousand dollars for the lot."

"There's certainly nothing here I'd sell in the shop," Arabella said, but she was already thinking two steps ahead. "Faye said she scoured the house for the desk key. If there was a will, she should have found it."

"Unless it was hiding in plain sight among a bunch of papers. I haven't found any paperwork up here, but I have yet to check the basement. I say we start there. After all, that's where Faye found the daguerreotype."

The daguerreotype. What if it was Alexander who'd hidden it in amongst the Christmas ornaments, and not Esther or Graham? Stanford had told her that Alex had become increasingly secretive. Her eyes landed on the stacking bookcase. Call it women's intuition, call it a hunch, but Arabella was sure she had the answer.

"Did you bring your laptop with you, Levon?"

"Yeah, why?"

"Because I think I might know where the will is hidden."

⬥

BACK AT THE KITCHEN TABLE, Arabella transferred the photographs from her camera to Levon's laptop, anxious to prove her theory. She clicked through them, pausing briefly to study each one, until finally making her selection. Once done, she zoomed in over the book in the young woman's hands, enlarged the title as far as she could, and slid the laptop over to Levon.

"*The Poetical Works of N.P. Willis*," Levon said. "Nathaniel Parker Willis. I've seen reproductions, but never the original. As I recall, it was first published by George Routledge and Sons in 1850, which makes it a good way to date the daguerreotype, but I'm not sure how this helps us in our search for the will."

"Don't you see? If I'm right, this volume is inside the bookcase. And somewhere inside the pages, we'll find Alexander Murdoch Gilroy's last will and testament."

⬥

THEY FOUND *The Poetical Works of N.P. Willis* on the third shelf. Levon went to his kit bag and took out a pair of white cotton gloves. "I was hoping there'd be some rare or antiquarian books, but I have to admit I wasn't expecting this," he said, pulling the gloves on, and removing the book. "Seriously, Arabella, the way your mind works never ceases to amaze me."

Arabella assumed Levon meant that as a compliment, but right now all that mattered was finding the will. She suggested as much to Levon, and was grateful when he agreed without any additional commentary.

Seated back at the table, Levon opened the book to the first poem, *The Healing of the Daughter of Fairus*. He began reading, his voice taking on the cadence of the long-dead poet.

"Freshly the cool breath of the coming eve
Stole through the lattice.
And the dying girl felt it upon her forehead. She had
  lain.
Since the hot noontide in a breathless trance—
Her thin, pale fingers, clasp'd within the hand of the
  heart-broken Ruler, and her breast,
Like the dead marble, white and motionless,
The shadow of a leaf lay on her lips,
And as it stirr'd with the awakening wind,
The dark lids lifted from her languid eyes,
And her slight fingers moved, and heavily
She turn'd upon her pillow. He was there—
The same loved, tireless watcher, and she'd looked
Into his face, until her sight grew dim,
With the fast-falling tears: and with a sigh
Of tremulous weakness murmuring his name,
She gently drew his hand upon her lips—"

"Enough already," Arabella said, not entirely sure why she'd interrupted at exactly that point in the poem, but determined to move forward. The last bloody thing she needed was Levon seducing her with sonnets. Or whatever this was.

Levon sighed. "You have to admit the prose is beautiful. Or have the years jaded your sense of romance?"

"Just because I don't want to listen to you spout nineteenth-century poetry doesn't make me jaded. We're looking for a will. Let's get on with it." Even as she said the words, Arabella regretted them. It wasn't that she didn't want to get on with it, but why did Levon have to make everything so complicated?

Levon, however, seemed to have moved on, his long fingers turning the pages carefully, the action interspersed with the occasional tut-tut of disapproval.

"I was afraid of this," he finally said, pointing out the reddish-brown spots, specks, and splotches on the pages. "A house as old as this one, humidity levels are bound to be inconsistent, and when books are improperly stored, foxing is almost certain to occur. True, most rare booksellers opt to leave well enough alone and simply strive to prevent further damage, but a skilled conservator can reverse foxing. There's been good, if not guaranteed success, with using a reducing agent, such as sodium borohydride, and—"

Borohydride, really? Who did he think he was talking to, a customer who didn't have a clue? True, he had more experience—and expertise—in collectible books than she did, but she'd handled enough of them that she didn't need a lecture.

"For heaven's sake, Levon, can you spare me the rhetoric?"

If she was expecting an argument or an apology, she didn't get it. Instead, Levon nodded and continued to carefully turn the brittle pages, until he came upon a single sheet of cream-colored paper, folded into quarters. He unfolded it with utmost care and smiled at Arabella, the rare, full-on one that transformed his features from studious to sensual.

"I think we just found the will, Bella baby."

24

THE DOCUMENT WAS HANDWRITTEN, the penmanship small and cramped, the letters a jumble of spiky peaks, thinly slashed t's, and uppercase E's and B's interspersed in the middle of many of the words. It was signed with a flourish by Alexander Murdoch Gilroy.

"It's a handwritten will, but it hasn't been witnessed. Is it legal?"

Levon was already searching on his laptop. "Handwritten wills are called holograph wills, and apparently they are quite common." He kept scrolling, then said, "There's a reference on the Ontario.ca website under the Succession Law Reform Act, section 6, Holograph Wills. 'A testator may make a valid will wholly by his or her own handwriting and signature, without formality, and without the presence, attestation, or signature of a witness.'"

Once again, Arabella was thinking about their next steps. Except…would Levon insist on taking this straight to a lawyer before they'd had a chance to read it? Not if she could help it.

She leaned forward, her green eyes locked into his blue ones. "What do you think we should do now? Call someone? Tell them what we've found? If so, who? A lawyer? Faye? Stanford? Or should we read the will first, and then decide our next steps?"

"I can't believe I'm saying this," Levon said, "but I vote for reading the will first."

"If you think that's best," Arabella said, suppressing a smile. It was the outcome she wanted, achieved without any bickering back and forth. It was the way you approached Levon that made all the difference, asking, never telling. If she'd learned nothing else in all the years she'd known him, she'd learned that.

🖎

DECIPHERING ALEXANDER MURDOCH GILROY'S handwriting had been a challenge, leaving both Levon and Arabella wondering what a handwriting analyst would make of it. Maybe they'd find out. It was a fair bet that an expert would be hired to validate the will's authenticity. Exactly who would do the hiring remained to be seen, especially given the contents. For a brief document, it packed a punch.

This is the last will and testament of Alexander Murdoch Gilroy. All previous wills and codicils are hereby revoked.

I, Alexander Murdoch Gilroy, being of sound mind and body, do hereby bequeath the property and contents of 21 Walnut Street, Lount's Landing, Ontario, to Esther Harriet Hadley, as a life interest, for her own use absolutely. Upon her death, ownership of the house and all contents will transfer to my son, Graham Alexander Gilroy. My remaining properties and assets, once liquidated, shall be split as follows: 25 percent to Esther Harriet Hadley, 25 percent to Kids Come First, Charitable Registration No. ON-5557676333, and 50 percent to my son, Graham Alexander Gilroy.

If he'd left it at that, nothing would have changed, outside of letting Stanford off the hook as executor. But of course, he wouldn't have made a new will if nothing else had changed. Arabella reread the final statement.

Under no circumstances should my daughter-in-law, Camilla Mortimer Gilroy, benefit in any way from my estate.

This holographic will is made entirely in my handwriting and made in two copies of equal substance.

Signed in Lount's Landing, Cedar County, Ontario, Canada, on the 14th Day of July, 1999. Alexander Murdoch Gilroy

"Two copies of equal substance," Arabella said. "That goes a long way to explaining why whoever took the trouble to hide this will didn't destroy it. Without a witness or a lawyer, it would have been easy enough to do, no one the wiser. But with a second copy floating around out there—"

"I knew Graham's folks didn't care for Camilla," Levon said, interrupting her, "but I never dreamed that his father hated her this much."

Arabella was about to voice her latest suspicion: that Alexander, and not Esther or Graham, had hidden both wills. Levon's interjection stopped her short. What if it had been Camilla who'd hidden the will *and* the daguerreotype? She didn't want to dredge up Levon's past history with Camilla, but this was no time to worry about her own insecurities.

"Did she say anything to you about why they felt that way?"

"Nothing beyond telling me that Alex and Rose never thought she was worthy of their son. According to Camilla, they made their feelings perfectly clear to anyone who was remotely interested. Which, in the case of this town, was pretty much everyone." Levon took Arabella's hand. "I know your loathing for Camilla runs deep, and that may or may not be warranted. But I can guarantee you that she was more than good enough for Graham. If it hadn't been for her business savvy, they would have lost the Gilroy Mansion, on top of everything else."

"It doesn't explain why Alexander wrote a holograph will or why he added the clause excluding Camilla."

"No, it doesn't. Not that it's any of our concern."

"But by inheriting this house from Graham, Camilla *did* benefit from Alexander's estate."

Levon frowned. "I'm not so sure. The wording could be construed as ambiguous."

"The will states, 'Under no circumstances should my daughter-in-law, Camilla Mortimer Gilroy, benefit in any way from my estate.' I'm not seeing the ambiguity."

"Once Alex's estate passed to his heirs, it would become part of their estate, would it not? In which case, Camilla could have legally inherited whatever Graham hadn't squandered. Including this house."

Levon had a point, though a lawyer might suggest otherwise. A lawyer representing…whom? If Graham couldn't bequeath anything inherited from his father to Camilla, who would benefit? Arabella had no idea, though Graham may have listed an alternate beneficiary in the event that he outlived his wife. Whatever the situation, a legal opinion was required, and the house would have to remain off the market until the matter was settled.

And what of the second copy? Could Stanford be the caretaker of that document, a detail so conveniently omitted in the telling of his tale? And if not Stanford, then who? More importantly, why hadn't that individual come forward? Surely they would have known the other copy would be discovered sooner or later.

The way Arabella figured it there was only one answer. They were waiting for something. What they were waiting for remained to be seen.

THEY AGREED TO SPLIT UP, Levon staying at the Hadley house to finish the appraisal, time being of the essence with this latest set of circumstances, and Arabella charged with finding a lawyer. *If*, and Levon had stressed the *if*, Arabella realized this was about getting a legal opinion, and not about her playing amateur detective. As *if* she didn't understand the seriousness of the situation.

She arrived back at the Glass Dolphin in short order, the walk calming her annoyance with her ex. The store already closed for the day, and with Emily long gone, Arabella checked the day's receipts —nothing beyond a rewired torchiere lamp—and settled into the task of looking for a lawyer. But how exactly did one go about doing that? She'd yet to draw up her own will, something she knew she should do. Well, this would be her opportunity, though googling "lawyers in Lount's Landing," seemed to lack due diligence. And did they even want to consult with a local lawyer? Attorney-client privilege aside, maybe it was better to turn to someone who had no prior knowledge of the Gilroys' money and their influence.

Money. Her friend, Callie Barnstable, had inherited a house in Marketville from her father back in 2016, albeit with some serious strings attached. And she'd recently inherited a sizable sum from her great-grandmother. Callie hadn't said how much money, but it was enough to bolster Callie's latest business initiative, Past & Present Investigations.

Arabella's knowledge of antiques had helped Past & Present delve into cold cases, including referring a Glass Dolphin customer as Callie's first client. Even Levon had gotten into the act when Callie needed information on vintage tattoo flash while searching for a young man who'd been missing for almost twenty years.

Arabella knew that the same lawyer had handled both estates, and furthermore, the inheritance from Callie's great-grandmother had widened the rift been Callie and her grandfather, as he'd expected to be the beneficiary. Which meant her lawyer was used to handling tricky situations.

Arabella couldn't remember his name. Had she ever known it? The obvious solution was to call Callie and ask, but the last thing she wanted was her friend horning in on the case.

Horning in on the case. Arabella almost laughed out loud. Levon, he knew her better than she knew herself. She picked up her phone and called Callie.

➤

"Leith Hampton," Callie said. "He's on Bay Street in Toronto, nice digs in the financial district. You won't find better, though you'll definitely find less expensive. Why do you find yourself in need of a lawyer who's good at handling tricky estate situations? Or should I ask?"

"It's not for me," Arabella said. "Levon and I have been hired to appraise the contents of the estate. The beneficiaries are adversarial, and things have gotten complicated. The executor has given us a very short timeline to sort things out."

If Callie wondered why two estate appraisers were commissioned with sorting things out and hiring a lawyer, she didn't say, though her lack of response spoke volumes.

"Leith Hampton, Bay Street," Arabella said into the silence. "I can look that up."

"No need." Callie rattled off the number. "Be sure to tell his assistant that you're a friend of mine. She's a formidable gatekeeper, and I suspect he's a bit of a snob when it comes to who he'll see."

"I will, and thank you."

"You can thank me by telling me what all this is actually about, when you're ready."

At least she didn't ask if we needed to hire her, Arabella thought and checked the time. She needed to reach Leith Hampton before he left for the day.

Leith Hampton's assistant was every bit the gatekeeper Callie said, grilling her like a seasoned PI, though the thaw was perceptible when the Barnstable name was dropped. "Let me discuss the matter with Mr. Hampton, see if he has any availability. I'll call you back shortly."

Arabella waited, willing herself to be patient. Thirty minutes later, her phone rang. "Mr. Hampton can see you at 11 a.m. tomorrow," the assistant said without preamble, her tone suggesting that Arabella take it or leave it, and that she was lucky at that. Arabella took it, even though it meant a last minute trip to the city when she'd hoped to do everything by phone. But a face-to-face meeting would be better, right?

She hung up, feeling good about the day until she checked her voicemail and texts. Four VMs and twice as many texts, all within the past three hours, all from Emily. Each one asking what the heck was going on with the Hadley house, though the language got stronger with each message.

Arabella sighed. Emily deserved the truth.

Or a sanitized version of it.

26

EMILY ANSWERED on the first ring. "It's about time,' she said, trying to keep the annoyance out of her voice, and not quite succeeding. "I've been trying to reach you all afternoon."

"I'm well aware," Arabella said drily. "The multiple texts and voicemail messages were a bit of a tip off."

"And yet you didn't answer."

"Only because I just now picked them up. I've been busy."

"Bob Wilkes told Poppy that executors are exercising extreme caution. Something about you and Levon finding a document in the Hadley house that requires further investigation?" Emily paused, waiting for Arabella to tell her more.

"Good try, but I can't tell you anything more. Levon and I signed a confidentiality agreement when we took on the estate appraisal."

"But I'm your business partner. You said yourself that the contract was with the Glass Dolphin. Surely that counts for something."

"No need to whine. You have an interest in the house, and I don't want you to jeopardize that. I've already shared more than I should have with you."

No need to whine? Shared with her? Like what, exactly? She had learned more from *Outside the Landing* than she had from Arabella. And, as much as she hated to admit it, once the house came back on the market, the deep pockets of Miles Pemberton and his production company would almost certainly be the winning bidder.

Miles Pemberton. Thinking of him reminded her of Sydney Van Fraassen. Maybe it was time to switch gears. "Sydney came by the shop today, brought me a smoothie, called it Blue Suede Shoes, blueberries, banana, peanut butter, and some other ingredients I can't remember. It was surprisingly good."

"That was nice of her." Arabella chuckled. "Maybe she read about your incident with Miles Pemberton on *Outside the Landing.*"

Emily had hoped Arabella hadn't heard about that. "Actually, she knew I had a bad cold, not that you've noticed." She sniffed loudly to emphasize the point.

"Sorry, I thought you sounded a bit stuffy, and to be honest, I haven't read the post yet. Stanford told me about it over dinner. But knowing Miles Pemberton, I'm sure he deserved whatever you dished out and then some."

Arabella had dinner with Stanford? Did he know about the mysterious document? Emily pushed the thought aside, knowing she wasn't going to get any answers, and said, "He did, and I'll fill you in on the sordid details over a drink sometime. Anyway, Sydney wasn't just bringing me a smoothie. When she was leaving she told me to find a way to beat Miles Pemberton at his own game. Do you know what she meant by that?"

"She *was* researching RV lifestyles when she was in Toronto for a series on the CKHTV network, though I don't think the project was green-lighted. Maybe Pemberton was involved. All I know is one day she was pumped about the project and the next day she was moving back to Lount's Landing to open a smoothie shop. But she clearly wants to talk about it, why not just ask her?"

"I don't want to seem nosey."

Arabella laughed. "When has that ever stopped you?"

"In that case," Emily said, "about the document you and Levon found—"

"Good night, Emily."

"Good night, Arabella." But Emily was smiling, a wave of optimism washing over her for the first time in days. Because Emily Garland, award-winning investigative journalist, was about to come out of retirement. And her first interview was going to be with Sydney Van Fraassen. Operation: Takedown Miles Pemberton was about to be set in motion.

27

___

Arabella arrived at the GO transit station with ten minutes to spare before the next train left to Toronto, relieved that she'd made the decision to walk the twenty minutes versus the quick five-minute drive. Since the introduction of reserved parking for regular commuters, spots for occasional commuters were sparse, and today, non-existent. There wasn't room in the lot for so much as a bicycle, let alone a car.

The trip from Lount's Landing to Toronto took just over an hour with multiple stops along the way, the train getting more and more crowded as they neared Union Station. Arabella had found a seat on the upper level's Quiet Zone, where she could read Levon's late night email. She'd phoned him after speaking to Emily, and let him know she was meeting with Leith Hampton. She expected some pushback, since she hadn't called someone local, but Levon agreed with her reasoning. She turned her attention to the email.

Hey Arabella,

As promised, I managed to finish the appraisal last night. Will write up the final report tomorrow. Not sure if you've finished writing up the history of Cutler Desk and daguerreotypes/reading dags? We should include both. If not,

I'll do it, just let me know. I just want get this done. I'm sorry I dragged you into it. I had no idea it would be so complicated.

Also, I didn't mention this last night, but I think it's best if we present the appraisal to Faye Everett together. We should probably tell her about the holograph will and whatever you learn from Hampton at the same time. Thoughts?

Good luck tomorrow, I'll be thinking of you.

Levon

Arabella had to smile at the "I'm sorry I dragged you into it." She'd never had so much fun doing an appraisal. She suspected Levon was trying to offer a subtle hint that he didn't want her mucking about with things once they'd met with Faye. Well, maybe she would, and maybe she wouldn't. It would all depend on what Leith Hampton told her. Along with the holograph will, she'd brought the will prepared by Joseph Fiorini.

She disembarked at Union and joined the throng of people making their way down to street level. It had been almost a year since Arabella had last been to Toronto, when she'd gone with Emily to see a matinee performance of *Come From Away* at the Royal Alexandra Theatre. The station had been under construction, a revitalization project that had swelled from a $600 million budget in 2014 to $840 million and counting. As she wound her way to the Bay Street exit, it appeared not much had changed.

Hampton & Associates was a short walk from Union, accessible from Bay Street or the PATH, a network of underground pedestrian tunnels and at-grade walkways that linked thirty kilometers of downtown offices, conference centers, restaurants, and shopping. Arabella had yet to use it without getting hopelessly lost. She opted for the great outdoors, amazed, as always, at the number of people coming and going, the had-to-be insane cyclists weaving their way in and out of gridlocked traffic. In the heart of Toronto's financial district, everyone was always in a hurry, even if getting somewhere in a hurry wasn't possible.

The law office was on the tenth floor, attractively furnished with a mix of mahogany and leather. Arabella introduced herself to a steely-eyed receptionist, and had no sooner taken a seat and picked up a *Bicycling* magazine when a faint scent of sandalwood wafted into the room. Arabella glanced up to see a slender man, about her height of five-foot-six, a slight paunch visible beneath the tailored suit jacket. Blue eyes, shrewd and intense.

"Leith Hampton," he said, a tail-wagging goldendoodle by his side. He leaned down to pat the dog and pulled a biscuit out of his pants pocket. "This is Atticus, my personal therapy dog. You must be Arabella Carpenter."

"Yes. Thank you for taking time out of your schedule to see me on such short notice."

"Two wills, one a holograph, both found hidden in a house you were hired to appraise. You piqued my interest. Besides, I feel as though I owe Calamity this favor." He led Arabella into a corner office. It wasn't particularly large, and you definitely got some street noise—horns honking, sirens, the occasional revving of a motorcycle engine —but it did offer a decent view of Bay Street.

Atticus took up residence in a chair by the corner. Going by the blanket that covered the fabric, this was his regular seat. A saltwater fish tank was on the wall opposite the window, the coral reefs, lava rocks, and lush vegetation artfully arranged. Arabella didn't know anything about fish or fish tanks, but she could imagine that watching the colorful aquatic scene could reduce stress after a hard day in court.

She took a seat across from Leith's desk, his telephone, tablet, and computer fighting for space among the overflowing manila file folders and stacks of paperwork.

"Organized chaos," Leith said, gesturing to the clutter without apology. "Now let's take a look at that holograph will."

28

———

Leith scanned the document quickly, nodding as he did so. "Signed *and* dated. The date is not strictly required by legislation in Ontario, but it does simplify things."

"Not strictly required?" Arabella shook her head. "How would one determine that it was actually the last will and testament?"

"A good question. In the case of an undated will, a judge is probably going to have to make a determination as to the validity, based on the best available evidence. Of course, in an estate with any significant assets, the will is going to be reviewed by a judge as part of the probate process to evaluate authenticity and validity. Perhaps the most famous example of an undated will, deemed valid, is that of Cecil George Harris, who, in June 1948, was pinned under his tractor on a farm near Rosetown, Saskatchewan. Fearing he may not survive, Harris used his pocketknife to scratch sixteen words onto the tractor's fender. 'In case I die in this mess I leave all to the wife. Cecil Geo Harris.'"

Leith leaned back in his chair as Arabella leaned forward. "It would be ten hours before help arrived to take Harris to the hospital. He died the next day from his injuries, never mentioning the will, which was discovered by neighbors. The fender was removed from the tractor and determined by the courts to be a valid holograph will. The fender was kept as evidence until 1996, when it was turned over to the University of Saskatchewan College of Law. It's still there, on public display."

"That's a great story," Arabella said, thinking she'd have to tell Levon about it.

"Most lawyers are born storytellers, though few of us have the gift of Grisham," Leith said with a smile. "But back to the reason you're here. It's important to note that a will, whether it be a holograph or otherwise, can be deemed invalid if the testator only 'wishes' to have his assets pass to the beneficiaries. The statement must be clear and unequivocal, such as 'I give,' or in the case of Alexander Murdoch Gilroy's will, 'I…do hereby bequeath.' One example of this distinction is the language used when the testator wants to leave direction regarding their remains. For instance, if someone wants to be cremated, we make the statement, 'It is my wish that I be cremated as opposed to buried' or something similar. In this case, the use of the word 'wish' is appropriate because, legally speaking, the estate's executor has the decision-making authority when it comes to how the remains are handled. The testator can do nothing more than express their wishes in this regard, rather than giving strict direction, as is necessary for the dispersion of their assets. By writing 'I…do hereby bequeath,' Alexander Murdoch Gilroy has given this strict direction."

"So this will would hold up in court?"

"Difficult to say. The two copies of equal substance could pose a legal issue."

"How so?"

"In general terms, only one will is considered to be valid. Even though they both might say 'made in two copies of equal substance,' without the second reportedly identical will to compare it to, a court might not validate the single copy. In other words, the reference to a second will might cause the court to deem the first will invalid. Do you know the whereabouts of the second copy?"

"I don't."

"I'd suggest you find it. Unless the second copy is found, it would be a very tricky argument on the part of the lawyer for the estate."

"Which would mean the will that predated the holograph would remain valid," Arabella said, and handed it over to Leith.

29

———————

Leith laid both wills side by side, comparing them line-by-line. It didn't take long.

"With the exception of removing Stanford McLelland as executor and the statement, 'Under no circumstances should my daughter-in-law, Camilla Mortimer Gilroy, benefit in any way from my estate,' the wording is identical," he said. "From that, one can make the assumption that Alexander Murdoch Gilroy wanted the will to hold up in court, and for reasons unbeknownst to us, he didn't want Stanford McLelland involved. Agreed?"

Arabella nodded.

"As I understand it, you and Mr. Larroquette were hired to appraise 21 Walnut Street, a house that formed part of Camilla Mortimer Gilroy's estate. I gather Camilla was Graham Gilroy's wife, and that he predeceased her."

Arabella nodded again.

"The statement excluding Ms. Gilroy is interesting," Leith said. "However, it is common for a will to include a clause which protects family assets from being diverted to others in the case of the separation or divorce of a beneficiary."

"But Graham and Camilla weren't separated or divorced at the time of his death," Arabella said, confused.

"The theory is the marriage was terminated by death. Even without a specific expression in Alexander's will, anything Graham inherited from his father would be deducted when determining Net Family Property—NFP—values under Ontario's Family Law Act."

Marriage terminated by death. Net Family Property. NFP. Ontario's Family Law Act. Arabella was beginning to feel snowed under. She pulled a notebook and pen out of her purse. "Can I take notes? I doubt I'll remember everything you're telling me."

Leith waited until Arabella was ready, then continued. "When two people enter into a marriage, each spouse is automatically entitled to an equal share of the profits of that marriage. That right to equalization is triggered, and the valuation date determined, when the marriage dissolves *or* one spouse dies. With me so far?"

Another nod. Arabella was beginning to feel like a bobble-head doll.

"When either occurs," Leith continued, "each partner becomes entitled to one half of the value of property accumulated *during* the marriage but, and this is important, not one half of the property itself. There's a formula involved under NFP, but essentially the court orders one spouse to pay the other an 'equalization payment,' so everything accumulated during the marriage is split fifty-fifty."

Marriage dissolves or one spouse dies

NFP

Accumulated during the marriage

Equalization payment, 50/50

The Gilroy Mansion had been in the family for three generations. Did that mean... She was about to ask Leith for clarification when he answered her question.

"The exception is the value of the matrimonial home, even if it was owned at the time of marriage. It is always included in the valuation date assets of the spouse who owns it."

"What if it's jointly owned?" Arabella asked, thinking of Luke and Emily and their plans to buy a house together.

"Then its value is divided equally between the spouses. This is the case even if the home was purchased with money inherited after marriage, or it was a gift to one of the spouses after marriage. Decisions such as whose name or names to put on the title, or whether or not to use money from an inheritance as a down payment, can have a dramatic impact..." Leith droned on as Arabella found herself zoning out. Until...

"Once Alexander's assets have been disbursed and his estate settled, the assets that Graham received are no longer Alexander's assets and no longer form part of Alexander's estate. As such, Alexander no longer has a say over how those assets are dealt with."

What? Good grief, she must have missed something important. "I'm sorry. What are you saying, exactly?"

"I'm saying that the courts do not allow people to reach out from the grave in order to control assets, once those assets have been disbursed."

Not being able to reach out from the grave. Camilla would have been disappointed to hear that, Arabella thought, *even if she was the one who would have lost out on an inheritance.* But something still niggled.

"Let me get this straight," she said. "Whether the will drawn up by Joseph Fiorini stands, or whether the holograph will is deemed valid—assuming the second copy of equal substance is found—nothing really changes."

"Right again, and sorry to disappoint, but...the law is the law. The statement prohibiting Camilla from benefiting could be considered a 'condition subsequent' and would therefore be struck down by the court. Even if Alexander's will said, 'fifty percent to Graham unless he shares it with Camilla,' the court would effectively cross out that condition."

"So if Graham left a will leaving everything to Camilla, including those assets received from his father, there would be nothing to prevent that from happening?"

"Exactly. Does that allay your concerns?"

"It does, thank you. I'll share everything I've learned with the executor. She may want to consult with her own lawyer, but hopefully the sale of the house can move forward as planned."

"There is one final point I'd like to make," Leith said.

"Yes?"

"We live in a litigious society. Should the second copy of the holograph will be discovered, and the contents disclosed, an unscrupulous lawyer might be persuaded to accept the case. They would lose in court, if it even got that far, but such action could serve to complicate or delay the sale of the house."

"Why would someone do that?"

Leith shook his head. "The motivation would have to be deeply personal. In other words, he or she would do whatever they could to uphold his Alexander's final wish, or go down trying."

30

FRIDAY MORNING AND OPERATION: Takedown Miles Pemberton was about to begin. Despite her lingering cold, Emily had never felt more ready for an assignment, even if she was the one doing the assigning. Arabella had booked the day off to go to Toronto, and based on the little she'd divulged, the trip had something to do with the Hadley house, but what? It was frustrating, not being in the know, but Emily knew better than to push her partner.

She had a lot to do and thankfully Caitie had agreed to cover for her at the shop. Her first stop was Sydney's Smoothie Bar, where Sydney Van Fraassen was wiping down an already gleaming stainless steel countertop when Emily knocked on the window.

"Emily, this is a pleasant surprise. I'm not open yet, but come on in, take a seat."

Sydney's Smoothie Bar was housed in a small, narrow space, with limited barstool seating at the front, and a half dozen round tables for four at the side. Posters of various anthropomorphic fruits and vegetables lined the walls, sporting captions like "Bananas are my favorite because they have appeal," "I-a-peach-iate you," "Simply Radishing," and "We're Root-ing For You," the latter a medley of smiling carrots, onions, beets, celery, and turnips.

"I take it the Blue Suede Shoes made a difference?" Sydney said.

"You know, I think it did. At any rate, my cold's on the mend."

"Happy to hear it. I was just about to make myself a breakfast smoothie. Care to split one with me? On the house. Unless you've already eaten?"

"Nothing. Just a cup of tea."

"How does a Wake Me Up Before You Go-Go Oatmeal smoothie sound?"

"I'll have Wham! earworm for the rest of the day. What's in it?"

"Organic rolled oats, banana, plain Greek yogurt, frozen mango, fresh strawberries, and enriched, unsweetened almond milk. It's incredibly nutritious. The oats are gluten-free and loaded with vitamins, minerals, and antioxidant plant compound, the banana adds potassium and a hint of sweetness, the yogurt supplies calcium and probiotics, mango aids in digestion and is a great source of vitamin C, the almond milk is low in calories and high in vitamin D, and strawberries add flavor, color, as well as manganese, which helps utilize protein, amino acid, and other vitamins and minerals while metabolizing cholesterol and carbohydrates."

Once again, Emily was impressed with Sydney's knowledge, and asked if she'd studied nutrition.

"I worked part-time for a nutrition center when I was going to Brock. The owner was into body building in a big way, but she also worked with distance runners and competitive swimmers. I made smoothies, transcribed her recorded consultations with the athletes, then entered them into a central database. It was interesting work, paid well, and the hours were flexible." Sydney grinned. "Of course, at the time I never dreamed I'd be running a smoothie shop in Lount's Landing, but life takes you where it takes you."

"That it does."

Sydney lined up the ingredients for the smoothie, measuring each one carefully before blending them together.

"Bottoms up," she said, handing Emily a glass.

Emily took a sip, then another. "It's delicious."

"One of my favorite recipes, not that I'm open for breakfast. I do well at lunchtime though, lots of students." She grinned. "Hence concoctions like the Tropical Rapini Rapper and Hip Hop Honeydew, not to mention the silly wall art. But the kids seem to like them."

Emily couldn't imagine drinking rapini, but marketing to the nearby high school kids was clever. "I never thought about trying to promote the Glass Dolphin to students. Do you think they might be interested?"

"I don't see why not. Your stuff is reasonably priced and would make unique gifts. Besides, antiques are green."

Emily laughed. "You've been listening to Arabella."

"And Levon," Sydney said, grinning. "As he says, 'Invest in the future and recycle the past.' But something tells me you didn't come here to discuss smoothies, students, or antiques. What's up?"

It was the perfect opening. "When you came by the shop yesterday, I was also left with the impression that you had more on your mind than delivering a blueberry smoothie."

Sydney blushed. "I suppose telling you to beat Miles Pemberton at his own game gave me away. I'm sorry, you don't need me complicating your life."

"On the contrary, I would love to beat Pemberton at his own game, and I need more ammunition." Emily explained how, after two months of searching, she and Luke had fallen for the Hadley house at first sight. "We're looking for a forever home, a place to raise kids. All Pemberton cares about is filming a renovation project and flipping it for a profit. Oh, I know, there's no law that prevents him from doing either, but…I don't know, it just doesn't seem fair."

"Pemberton never plays fair. Knowing how much you want the house will only make him want to win, no matter what. Winning is everything to him."

Emily was surprised at the bitterness in Sydney's voice. However Pemberton had wronged Sydney, she was far from over it. "What did he do to you?"

"Did you read the report in *Outside the Landing*, the one about a TV show called *House Haunters*?"

"I did. And I thought the anonymous source was Pemberton,

trying to spook anyone who might be interested in the Hadley house."

"I couldn't agree more. Whoever Truth Seeker is, she's right about *Pemberton on Property* being on life support. Ratings last year plummeted, especially in the Adults 18-49 demographic. That's meaningful because it's the target demo that sets ad rates for entertainment programming."

"It *was* a dull season," Emily said. "Like Pemberton and the producer had run out of ideas."

"He'd never admit that. He laid the blame squarely on the shoulders of the show's researcher for not finding him good properties, even though he had final say on each and every property selected. And he selected several properties against her advice. Miles Pemberton is never wrong. If a lowly researcher's good name was destroyed in the process, so be it."

"I read in *Inside the Landing* that you'd been a freelance researcher for a number of home-improvement programs on the CKHTV network. Were you the researcher for *Pemberton on Property*?"

"Yes, though I worked on a number of shows for the network before being handpicked for *P on P* last season. I had doubts about taking the job. I'd developed a solid reputation and there were rumors that *P on P* was tanking. And I didn't trust Pemberton. He has one face for the camera and another behind the scenes."

"I know the type," Emily said, thinking about Garrett Stonehaven, an unscrupulous developer who had everyone fooled with his seemingly altruistic HavenSent Development scheme. She'd been sent to report on HavenSent by then-boss Michelle Ellis and *Urban Living Publications*. The investigation was what had initially brought her to Lount's Landing.

She nodded at Sydney. "Let me guess, they appealed to your ego and your pocketbook."

"The money was double my usual rate, and I'll admit to being flattered. Who wouldn't be? Even so, I might not have taken the gig if it hadn't been for Megan."

"Megan?"

Sydney nodded. "Megan Sutcliffe, the executive producer. We were roommates in university."

Megan Sutcliffe. The same woman who, at least according to *Outside the Landing*, stood to inherit 21 Walnut Street. And now Miles Pemberton was looking to buy the property.

31

———

Emily chose her words carefully. The last thing she needed was Sydney getting defensive about her friend. "Megan Sutcliffe. Isn't that the woman mentioned in *Outside the Landing?* The one Truth Seeker claims will inherit the Walnut Street house?"

"One and the same," Sydney said, "and I know what you're thinking. But let me tell you that in addition to being roommates, I thought Megan and I were friends. I was wrong."

"You blame Megan for talking you into the research job for *Pemberton on Property.*"

"If only it was that simple. Unfortunately it runs deeper than that. At the time Megan approached me, I'd been writing a treatment for a new series, one that followed folks who'd embraced an RV lifestyle. I was just about ready to pitch it to the network. I envisioned being hired on as producer, even winning an Emmy or two." Sydney laughed. "Hey, dream big or go home, right?"

"There's nothing wrong with dreaming big," Emily said.

"Except when dreams come back to break your heart. I'd spent months on the project, interviewing potential candidates, and I'd finally found the perfect couple, Paul and Louise. They were empty nesters, their three adult children scattered across the country. The plan was to simplify their life, sell the house and its contents, and use the money to travel across North America, no real schedule, just stopping and staying a while, then moving on when the mood struck them. They called their RV the Taj Mah Paul. Clever, right?"

"Very," Emily said.

"You're probably wondering how this relates back to Megan. The long and the short of it is that I trusted her, even when I knew better."

"Was she untrustworthy?"

"Not to me, though in school I heard she'd take credit for team project ideas that weren't hers. Of course, she'd deny it and tell me the other students were jealous of her because of her father's money."

"Did you believe her?"

"At first, yes. She's smart, beautiful, and she never put up with anyone's crap, which I admired. But then she landed a full-time paid internship working with Miles Pemberton at CKHTV after graduation. The most the rest of us could hope for was a low-paying, most likely unpaid internship, deep in the trenches. But paid? With a name brand like Pemberton? Definitely someone pulling strings. I suspect that someone was Dwight Sutcliffe, though whether he had dirt on Pemberton or covertly funded her salary is anyone's guess. And if I'm being honest, I hoped she'd get me into the network, too. And she did, as a freelance researcher."

"So you owed her, or thought you did."

"Yeah. When she practically begged me to take on the head researcher role at *Pemberton on Property*, I told her that I wasn't sure. Not because of Miles Pemberton, even though that was definitely part of it, but because I was working on a project of my own. And then I told her about Paul and Louise. She said all the right things. That it was brilliant, my time to shine, long overdue, promised to connect me with the right people, and help pitch the show to the execs. I'd be named as the content creator."

"I take it that didn't happen."

"Not a single connection, but I didn't worry, at least not at first. Networking opportunities can take time to set up. But as the days on

Pemberton on Property turned into weeks, I began to wonder if she'd come through. And then word leaked about Megan's latest hot project, *Reality RV: Live Free and Drive*." Another humorless laugh. "I wouldn't be surprised if she leaked the news herself."

"Did you confront her?"

"I tried. She said I told her to pitch the idea to the executives.

"And had you?"

"Yes, but with me listed as the concept creator. When I asked her if she'd done that, she admitted she hadn't. Her excuse was Pemberton had been dissatisfied with my work. Megan claimed if my name was attached to it, the project would never get off the ground, but she had my back." Sydney shook her head. "More like a knife in my back. The last two episodes of *Pemberton on Property* had been a ratings disaster, but I wasn't the researcher on them. Megan knew that."

"What did you do?"

"What could I do? Go to the executives and tell them Megan had stolen my idea? How was I going to prove it? Who'd take my word over hers, especially with her father's influence? And then, to add insult to injury, Miles Pemberton fired me."

"Do you think Megan was behind that, too?"

"I blamed her at first, but I don't know. Megan is ambitious, but until then, she'd been a loyal friend. After Pemberton let me go, the network suggested that I take a six-month sabbatical. I took my savings, what was left of my pride, my knowledge of nutritional science, and came back to Lount's Landing. Poppy Spencer is a friend of my mom's. She found this spot and I went into the smoothie business."

"Where is Megan now?"

"I've seen her out and about, not that I've spoken to her. You've probably seen her, too. It's a small town, after all."

Emily couldn't recall seeing any strangers wandering about. "What does she look like?"

"Late twenties, killer body, pale complexion, dark eyes, and very distinctive cherry bomb red hair. Dyed, of course."

Cherry bomb red hair. Emily thought back to the attractive redhead in a black power suit, her attitude patently professional when she'd met outside with Jay Mulacki and Miles Pemberton. Professional, but definitely not submissive. So *that* was Megan Sutcliffe.

"As a matter of fact, I have seen her," Emily said.

"Call me naive," Sydney said, "but I doubted the *Outside the Landing* story about Megan's conflict of interest regarding the Hadley house. Megan may be ruthlessly ambitious, but she's not stupid. She would never knowingly get involved in anything that smelled of conflict of interest."

"So you think there's more than a reality TV show going on here," Emily said.

"They're actually referred to as 'docudramas' now, so much more dignified, don't you think?" Sydney said, grinning. "But, to answer your question, yes, I think there's more going on than meets the eye. But what? I don't know. I do believe that all roads lead back to Miles Pemberton."

"Which brings me back to the reason I'm here. If I can prove that Pemberton is doing something illegal, heck, even if I can prove all he's doing is verging on unethical, then surely the sellers won't accept any offer he makes on 21 Walnut Street. With the Pemberton Productions money out of the running, Luke and I stand a fair chance to get the property for a fair price. If we still lose it in a bidding war, so be it. But at least we'd have a shot at it."

"Then the two of us will have to figure out a way to beat him together, won't we?" Sydney said, a steely glint in her eyes. "I'll get my reputation back and you'll get your house."

"What about the smoothie bar?"

"Who knows? Maybe it'll make a great docudrama. In fact, I can already envision my pitch."

32

———

Arabella texted Levon as soon as she'd settled into the Quiet Zone of the train. *"You were right."* It irked her to admit it, but she'd have to tell him sooner or later. May as well be sooner.

He was back to her within seconds. *"About?"*

"Camilla inherits. Set up Sat. meeting with Faye."

That netted her a thumbs up emoji and a *"Not often you tell me I'm right. Saving the text in case it doesn't happen again."*

She clicked off her phone, smiling, and went over her notes, adding questions as she did so.

- Who has the second copy of the holograph will and why haven't they come forward?
- Did Graham have an alternate beneficiary in the event Camilla didn't survive him?
- Why did Alexander remove Stanford McLelland as executor?

She leaned back into her seat. All good questions, but how was she going to get the answers?

◄●

IF STANFORD HAD BEEN curious about another meeting with her so soon after the last, he didn't question it, and Arabella was grateful. She arrived ten minutes late, apologetic for the delay.

"I'm so sorry. I've been in Toronto all day. Had to go home, take a quick shower, and change. I should have said 5:30."

"No apology necessary. What business took you to Toronto? Auction? Estate sale?"

"None of the above. It was the Hadley house. Or rather what Levon and I discovered there." Arabella started at the point where they'd discovered the holograph will, and concluded with her consultation with Leith Hampton.

"All very interesting," Stanford said after she'd finished. "Where do I fit in?"

"I thought you might be the person Alexander entrusted with the second copy of the holograph will."

"I knew he'd made another will, just as I told you," Stanford said, not quite meeting Arabella's gaze. "I didn't know it was a holograph, and I didn't know the contents."

"But you know more than you've told me." Arabella smiled. "We worked together for years, and I can tell you're holding something back."

That netted her an exaggerated sigh, then, "I know why Alex removed me as executor. But it wasn't relevant. You and Levon were hired to appraise an estate, not to play amateur detective. Do you see yourself as the last vestige of hope in honoring Alex's final wishes?"

"Perhaps. What aren't you telling me?"

"Alex found out I'd become friends with Camilla. He couldn't forgive that."

Arabella's eyebrows shot up. "Friends?"

Stanford flushed. "Maybe more than friends."

"Are you saying that you and Camilla were having an affair?"

"You make it sound so tawdry."

"She was the wife of your best friend's son. It doesn't get much more tawdry than that."

"In my defense, Camilla told me their marriage was in serious trouble. That they were planning to separate."

Arabella was about to ask if that was before or after Stanford had slept with her. But then a thought crossed her mind. "Had they drawn up a legal separation agreement?"

Stanford nodded. "She was quite incensed about it, felt that Graham was trying to screw her over for what was rightfully hers. Her words, not mine." He gave a rueful smile. "But then Alex died and Camilla and Graham reconciled. She told me she was staying with Graham because he was grieving the death of his father. I had no reason to doubt her. "

"And now?"

"I don't know what to believe, though I expect she knew about the holograph will. It was the sort of thing Alex would have lorded over her with glee. Either way, as you said yourself, it hardly matters. The dead can't reach out from the grave. Not even someone as powerful as Alexander Murdoch Gilroy." Stanford glanced at his watch. "Now it's my turn to apologize. I have a client coming in a few minutes."

↩

BACK HOME, Arabella changed into plaid flannel PJ pants, an oversized tee, and a polar fleece hoodie. She made herself a cup of tea and began reviewing her notes.

Marriage terminated by death
Net Family Property, NFP
Ontario's Family Law Act
Marriage dissolves or one spouse dies
Accumulated during the marriage but not one half of the property
Equalization payment.

Accumulated during the marriage but not one-half of the property. Which meant that if Camilla and Graham had been legally separated at the time of his death, Camilla would not have inherited any property owned by Graham before their marriage.

That would explain their reconciliation. Because Arabella was certain that Alexander had told Camilla about the clause specifically excluding her in his holograph will. He may even have shown it to her. She could imagine him flaunting it in her face, triumphant.

Gotcha.

She googled, "What if a couple reconciles after separating?"

The answer was crystal clear. Most standard separation agreements in Ontario included a clause stating if the parties cohabited for ninety days or more, including non-consecutive periods, the terms of their separation agreement would immediately become void.

There was a catch, however. According to one website, "any payments, conveyances, or acts, including property transfers made or done pursuant to the terms of the separation agreement, would remain valid, even though the agreement itself would be invalidated."

Arabella called Stanford. He answered on the first ring, his tone more cautious this time than in the past, a fact she deeply regretted. "One more question," she said. "If you have time."

"I'll do my best to answer," he said, and Arabella's heart broke at the formality in his voice. She swallowed hard, knowing the answer to her next question was important. Hoping that her relentless digging hadn't cost her Stanford's friendship.

"About Camilla," she said. "Do you know if she received any money or property from Graham as part of a legal separation agreement?"

A long pause and then, "To the best of my knowledge, they reconciled before she ever saw a dime, something that undoubtedly haunted her until the day she died. But it was the only way Graham would take her back." Stanford let out a humorless laugh. "Camilla always did have her eye on the end game."

She did indeed. Despite Alexander's best efforts, Camilla had managed to get the last laugh. A part of Arabella almost admired her.

33

The subterfuge started off as Sydney's idea, though it hadn't taken much to get Emily on board. Emily wanted Pemberton publicly humiliated and fired from CKHTV. So did Sydney, though she also wanted the same fate for Megan. "Karma," was the way she had put it.

All Emily knew was that with Pemberton Productions out of the picture, she and Luke would have a shot at buying the Hadley house, if and when it came back on the market. And so she'd agreed to the plan: Sydney would call Megan under the guise of mending fences and ask to meet her at The Hanged Man's Noose that evening to discuss a matter of importance to both of them. Unbeknownst to Megan, Sydney would bring Emily along as a friend and journalist who was writing an article about Miles Pemberton.

What kind of article? Emily needed a backstory. An exposé, but about what? And who would publish it? Miles Pemberton had a huge fan base; any reputable publication would shy away. Scrap that idea. What if she was writing a story about house hunting with her fiancé, and her experience running up against Miles Pemberton? Admit that she knew Megan was on the *P on P* team, and was hoping to get some inside scoop. It could work…as long as Megan didn't have an aversion to journalists. But she was in television, right? Surely she was used to being interviewed.

To Sydney's surprise, Megan seemed to welcome the invitation to meet at the Noose for drinks later that evening.

"Maybe she's got a guilty conscience," Emily said.

"I'll believe it when I see it," Sydney replied. "Knowing Megan, she's figured out an angle for herself. The woman is too clever by half."

"Then we'll have to be more clever by full," Emily said. After all, when it came to playing angles, she had first-hand experience.

Megan was already seated at a round table by the window, a glass of red wine in front of her, when Sydney and Emily arrived at The Hanged Man's Noose. She stood up and waved at Sydney, a puzzled look crossing her face when she saw Emily. Megan's black power suit had been replaced with a thigh-length hunter green sweater and stylishly ripped jeans, the cherry bomb red hair left loose and flowing in waves past her slender shoulders. It made her look younger, more vulnerable. The cynic in Emily wondered if it was a deliberate calculation, a way to put Sydney off her guard.

"Megan, thanks for agreeing to meet with me," Sydney said. "This is my friend, Emily Garland. She's a journalist."

Megan's brow furrowed in concentration. "I recognize you from somewhere…wait a second. You're the one who was looking at 21 Walnut Street at the same time as Pemberton and Mulacki. Your realtor is…Petunia?"

"Poppy. Poppy Spencer, the number one agent in the tri-communities, despite what Bob Wilkes might have told you." Emily wasn't sure why she added that last bit. A weak attempt at intimidation? Or because she it was likely Megan knew not only Poppy's name, but also her reputation?

"Right, Poppy. My mistake," she said with a casual shrug. "So it *was* you that I saw?"

"It was."

"And you were also the one who tore into Pemberton at the dollar store?"

"Guilty as charged."

A brief smile, then, "I might have paid to see that."

"I thought you and Pemberton were tight," Sydney said.

"Appearances can be deceiving. You've been around reality TV long enough to know that." Megan studied Emily. "Sydney introduced you as a journalist. I thought you co-owned an antiques shop."

"You seem to know a lot about me."

"Local antiques shop co-owner throws a hissy fit," Megan said, quoting *Outside the Landing*.

"Right. I've been trying to forget about that."

Another brief smile. "I'm sure you have, along with all the other vitriolic posts written about you and your partner. Whoever Truth Seeker is, they're definitely not a fan of yours."

"Let's just say we have a history."

Megan's eyebrows shot up. "You know the identity of Truth Seeker?"

"I can make an educated guess. But I won't tell you who I think Truth Seeker is in the event I'm wrong."

"Fair enough. So tell me, how does an antiques shop owner transform herself into an investigative journalist?"

"Actually it's the other way around. I came to Loun's Landing on an assignment and decided to stay." Emily didn't think Megan needed to know why. She shifted a bit in her chair and thankfully Betsy took that moment to swing by their table—subliminal message received? Or a bartender used to reading body language? Either way, Emily was thankful.

Drinks ordered and delivered—another glass of red for Megan, house white for both Sydney and Emily—Megan turned her focus to Sydney.

"You told me that you had a matter of some importance to discuss. Then you bring a journalist with you. Which leads me to ask: What is Emily writing about?"

"Miles Pemberton."

"You have my attention," Megan said.

34

"I'm sure you know that 21 Walnut Street has been taken off the market," Sydney began.

"A temporary situation that has absolutely nothing to do with Miles Pemberton or me, despite the implication in *Outside the Landing* that I was involved in a conflict of interest," Megan said. "My understanding is that offer day will almost certainly take place next week, probably Monday."

"Far be it for me to take the side of *Outside the Landing*," Emily said, "but my understanding is that you are the executive producer for *Pemberton on Property* and a beneficiary under Camilla Mortimer-Gilroy's estate, which includes 21 Walnut Street. That could be viewed as a conflict of interest."

"All true, if Pemberton's interest in the house is for an episode of *P on P*. That isn't the case. He is considering the property for a new series tentatively titled *House Haunters*. The network has since made it clear I won't be involved in that production."

Was that a trace of bitterness Emily heard in Megan's voice? Emily glanced at Sydney, who gave her a barely perceptible nod. "Was that before or after I saw you talking to Jay Mulacki and Pemberton outside the house?"

For the first time, Megan flinched. "It was after that."

"So at the time, you believed you would be part of the program?"

"Yes, but it's not what you think. I went to the house that day to inform Pemberton of my status as beneficiary. We all agreed it would be best if I stepped aside because of the optics, and because I wasn't willing to risk an inheritance for the sake of a television show. Unfortunately, the article in *Outside the Landing* made me sound duplicitous. The network executives got wind of it somehow and…" Megan's voice broke. "It wasn't a pleasant conversation."

"You think Pemberton was behind the leak," Emily said.

Megan nodded. "Nothing I can prove, of course. I still have a job at CKHTV, but my future there is tenuous. So is the series I had in the pipeline."

"The one about the RV lifestyle?" Sydney asked with a trace of satisfaction.

Megan blushed. "Yeah. And not just because of the blog post. The retired couple, Paul and Louise, the ones with the Taj Mah Paul? They threatened to pull out of the pilot unless you're rehired. Apparently you remind them of their daughter in Calgary."

"Funny, I don't recall getting a phone call from the network," Sydney said. "I think I would have remembered that."

The blush deepened. "The network was unaware of your involvement in the project. I did a bit of fancy footwork, told them you were enjoying your sabbatical, that you'd set up a successful smoothie shop in Lount's Landing. They encouraged me to persuade you to come back. I've spent the last three days trying to think of a way to approach you. Your call came at an opportune time."

"Always willing to make your life easier," Sydney said, her voice dripping with sarcasm.

"I deserved that."

"You did," Sydney said, but there was a hint of a smile. "I do have a question, though. What if I don't come back and Paul and Louise actually withdraw their participation in the project? What happens to the show then?"

"I don't know about the show, but I'd almost certainly be parting ways with CKHTV. My father's influence only stretches so far, and that's just as well. I've done so many things wrong in my life, knowing he'd be there to bail me out, starting with the way I treated my sister, Faye. What a mess I made of that relationship. And you, Syd, I'm so sorry. You deserve a better friend than me. Sometimes my ambition clouds my better judgement. But I never thought you'd get fired, you have to believe that. That was all Miles Pemberton. He needed a scapegoat because *P on P* was failing. You were in the wrong place at the right time."

"A wrong place that you convinced me to go to," Sydney said, her expression hard.

"Also true, but I truly believed it could open doors for you. I never thought it would close them. You do believe me, don't you?"

Sydney nodded. "I do. And it sounds as if your ambition might have cost you your career. That's a high price to pay."

"Are you saying you forgive me? That you'll come back?"

"Forgive you? It's a bit too soon for that. As for coming back, I have the smoothie bar to consider. What if I close up shop, and *Reality RV* doesn't pan out?"

"I can't promise it will pan out, at least not long term, you know that. There are never any guarantees in television. But I can assure you the network has committed to thirteen episodes, initially, if you're on board. As for the smoothie bar, surely you can hire someone to manage it, at least for the time being."

Sydney's gaze cut to Emily, who was nodding her encouragement. Thought about Paul and Louise, how they'd backed her, even when she wasn't there. "Okay. You can tell the network I'll come back. On three conditions."

"Name them."

"I'm listed, along with you, as an executive producer on *Reality RV: Live Free and Drive.*"

"Done."

"And I get top billing."

"Goes without saying. And the other condition?"

Sydney nodded towards Emily. "We want you to ensure that Miles Pemberton doesn't buy the Walnut Street house."

"I'm not sure I can prevent that from happening," Megan said. "The bank has the final say. Besides, unless there are some crazy conditions attached, the top bid will almost certainly win. And Pemberton Productions has—or had, emphasis on the *had*—very deep pockets."

"What do you know that we don't?" Sydney asked.

Megan leaned forward and dropped her voice to a whisper. "Pemberton's budget is half of what it usually is."

"Does that mean Pemberton doesn't have the budget to buy the Hadley house?" Emily asked.

"Maybe."

Emily considered that before saying, "We're not asking you to do anything unethical or illegal. We want Pemberton to walk away. If there's public humiliation or job loss as a result, all the better."

"So much for not holding a grudge," Megan said.

"This isn't about holding a grudge," Sydney said. "It's about making sure Pemberton gets what he deserves."

"A convenient distinction, but, given the target, one I can buy into." Megan studied Emily with narrowed eyes. "I'm assuming you and Syd have a plan?"

Emily nodded. "We do."

35

Levon arrived at the Glass Dolphin at seven o'clock Saturday morning. "You should be back in plenty of time to open the store at eleven," he said, handing Arabella a small paper bag and a large takeout coffee. "Courtesy of the Sunrise Café. One sugar, extra cream in the coffee. Toasted cinnamon raisin bagel with peanut butter. I figured you would have skipped breakfast. I assume it's still your favorite?"

"I did and it is, thank you, much appreciated." Arabella said. She summarized her consultation with Leith, outlining the various scenarios, and finished with a recap of her meeting with Leith.

"Whoa," Levon said when she'd finished. "Stanford and Camilla?"

"I wonder if Graham knew or suspected."

"The only people who know are dead, not that it matters. The affair was over long before Graham crashed through the ice on his snowmobile. Camilla can be blamed for many things, but I don't think we can pin his death on her."

"I wasn't suggesting that," Arabella said, though the thought had crossed her mind. "Regardless, we can tell Faye that we've checked out every angle and that she can safely put the house back on the market. I suppose we'll have to hand over the holograph will as part of the estate, but I don't think she needs to know her aunt cheated on her uncle."

"Agreed, there'd be nothing to gain by doing so."

Arabella handed Levon a two-page document. "I've prepared a write-up on estate law to include with our appraisal. It's written in layman's terms, with website links to the Ontario legislation and lawyers specializing in that arena. I thought it best to be thorough."

"Good work."

"Thanks. It was eye-opening, to say the least. I'm going to have a long talk with Emily."

"I don't understand. You don't think her marriage to Luke will last?"

"That's not what I said. I think they're perfect for each other. Today. But everyone goes into marriage thinking it will last forever. Statistics prove otherwise." *Our own situation proves otherwise*, Arabella thought, but didn't say. She switched the subject. "Have you finished writing up the appraisal?"

"Yup. Books, paintings, furniture, including the history of the Cutler Desk Company and, thanks to your extensive notes, daguerreotypes. A few saleable items, but nothing of great value, though I did find an interesting book titled *The American Daguerreotype* by Floyd and Marion Rinhart, published in 1981. Not super old, but worth three or four hundred dollars to the right collector." Levon produced a yellowed receipt. "This was inside it. Interesting, to say the least."

The receipt was handwritten in turquoise ink, Kit Kat Antiques & Curiosities, Toronto, stamped at the top. It was made out to E. Hadley and dated July 21, 1999. "One box Shiny Brite Christmas ornaments, ca. 1955. Girl with book sixth-plate daguerreotype, ca. 1850."

"I couldn't find a Kit Kat Antiques in Toronto online," Levon said, "but it's interesting that Esther purchased the ornaments and the dag at the same time."

"It's more than interesting," Arabella said, studying the receipt. "What do you mean?"

"Alexander's holograph will was dated July 14, 1999. Esther made this purchase exactly one week later, almost certainly with the plan to hide the dag in the ornament box. Only she could have tucked this receipt inside a book. No one else would have had a reason to do that. And if she used the book to keep the receipt, it stands to reason she would have used a book to hide the holograph will. Alexander must have told her to keep it in a safe place in the event someone destroyed the other copy."

"Someone being either Graham or Camilla," Levon said.

"Exactly, though my money would be on Camilla. She would have almost certainly known about the will we found in the desk, because Stanford would have told her, not that he'll ever admit it."

"Pillow talk."

"Exactly. Stanford was also sure she knew about the holograph will, said it was the sort of thing Alexander would have gleefully lorded over her. What if he handed it to her, feeling oh-so-clever about the copy of equal substance, unaware of the legal complications such a statement would create?"

"Knowing Camilla, she would have gotten legal advice, especially after Alexander died," Levon said. "And the best advice would have been to dump Stanford and reconcile with Graham."

"Which," Arabella said, "is exactly what she did."

"Learning about her affair with Stanford, the talk of separation…I didn't understand, before, why Alexander hated Camilla enough to exclude her from inheriting. But it makes sense now. He was only trying to protect his son."

"It goes to prove one thing," Arabella said.

"What's that?"

"All the money in the world can't buy happiness."

36

———————

ARABELLA AND LEVON met Faye at the Hadley house at eight-thirty, allowing Arabella plenty of time to open the Glass Dolphin at eleven.

Faye didn't waste time on pleasantries once they'd taken their seats at the kitchen table. "Can we put the house back on the market?"

Levon nodded. "Yes, you can, and with a clear conscience." He handed the holograph will over to Faye, sharing the steps they'd taken to find it, his pride in Arabella's deductions evident. "Yesterday, Arabella went to see Leith Hampton, a well-respected Toronto lawyer. She took both wills with her."

"I've summarized my consultation with Leith in a word document," Arabella said. "I've also included links to websites that I found helpful, as well as lawyers specializing in estate law if you want to consult one of your own. The bottom line is the law doesn't allow the dead to reach out from the grave. Therefore, when Alexander died, this house was bequeathed to Esther Harriett Hadley, but only as a life interest. When she died, Graham inherited it. And, when he died, with Camilla as his beneficiary, she inherited, and subsequent to her death, you and your stepsister inherited."

"Impressive," Faye said, scanning the document. "Though I expect not being able to reach from the grave would have been a disappointment to Aunt Cam."

Arabella suppressed a grin, knowing she'd had the same thought. "I did have one question for you. Do you know if Graham's will had an alternate beneficiary in the event Camilla predeceased him?"

"Yes. Megan and I stood to inherit, as they didn't have children of their own. At least that's what Aunt Cam told us. I never saw the actual will, and I doubt that Megan did either. We weren't super close, but we were family. Why, does it matter?"

"If I'd thought to ask before, we wouldn't have been concerned about the exclusion of Camilla in the holograph will. Because either way, you and Megan would have inherited this house."

"I guess you're right. But I'm glad that you went to a lawyer. Aunt Cam was a piece of work, but she was our piece of work. I like to think she inherited everything fair and square. And whatever her faults, she was devoted to Uncle Graham. She was inconsolable after he died."

Levon glanced at Arabella, and she knew that he was thinking about Camilla's affair with Stanford. Thankfully, they'd agreed there was no point in sharing that bit of news. *Rest in peace, Camilla,* Arabella thought, and was surprised to realize she actually meant it. If nothing else, this process was helping her to let go of the past. Whatever animosity she'd felt towards Camilla had dissipated, and the lingering doubts she'd had about Levon's relationship with Camilla no longer seemed important.

Faye interrupted her thoughts. "What about the appraisal? Has it been completed?"

"All in this binder," Levon said, sliding it across to her. "Everything in the house has been itemized, along with historical context, where applicable, estimated values and reasons for those estimates, as well as suggestions on how to best liquidate. Unfortunately, there isn't anything in the house that will make you rich, and most is best donated to a charity shop. Some will provide tax receipts, but not all. At any rate, it's all in there, and you know where to find us if you have any questions. And we can certainly put you in touch with potential buyers."

"We're also willing to purchase some things for a fair price," Arabella said. "There's a book of poetry that Levon would love, for example."

"And one on daguerreotypes that would be a welcome addition to the Glass Dolphin's research materials," Levon added. "Not to mention the reading dag."

"And then there's the desk," they said at the same time, then acted out a mock competition of rock, paper, scissors, laughing like two kids as they did it.

Faye grinned. "You two really *are* better than a Hallmark movie."

37

Saturday morning arrived and despite the suggestion of a hangover, Emily was primed for Operation: Takedown Miles Pemberton. The wine had been flowing the night before, and she'd swapped stories with Megan and Sydney, starting with the way Poppy Spencer had spent months working with Pemberton, only to learn he'd hired Jay Mulacki to find a property for *House Haunters*.

"He didn't even have the decency to give Poppy a heads up," Emily told them. "She found out when we went to view the property and Pemberton showed up with Mulacki. He claimed the network signed an exclusive agreement with Jay for all their real estate holdings and that he had no say in the matter."

"Phooey," Megan had said. "Any agreement would have been signed on behalf of Pemberton Productions, of which Miles is CEO."

"That's exactly what I thought."

It was apparent that Pemberton had screwed over everyone he'd worked with. By the time the three of them had piled into a shared taxi, their cars left in the parking lot behind the bar, they were sisters in solidarity, with a list of others they hoped to recruit.

Miles Pemberton wasn't going to know what hit him.

HER CAR still at the Noose, and thankful that her cold had been reduced to mildly annoying, Emily walked to the Sunrise Café. She needed a breakfast of grease to offset the burgeoning hangover, and the café would be full of gossip.

The Sunrise Café was housed within a narrow, brown brick Victorian. A brass historical plaque indicated the building was once the establishment of Murdoch Gilroy, Esquire, the front door painted a bright, sunshiny yellow. Emily pulled on a brass handle and made her way inside, a wash of memories flooding over her. Five years ago, this had been her first stop in Lount's Landing. So much had changed in her life since that day, but inside the restaurant, time had stood still. It was charming in a country-cozy way, with colorful prints of roosters and other farm life adorning the walls. Overhead, ceiling fans with alternating blades of bright yellow and orange spun lazily, circulating the smell of coffee, cinnamon, and buttered toast. Emily sat down at a table for two by the window, no longer a stranger in town, but one of the locals.

Or at least local-ish, Emily thought with a grin. You'd have to run at least one generation deep before you were accepted completely. But it would be a good place to raise a family with Luke.

Luke. He probably wouldn't approve of Operation: Takedown Miles Pemberton. Just as well he was busy at the trade show in Toronto. She'd fill him in…later.

There were two servers on duty, a young woman Emily didn't recognize—Saturday student help could be a bit of a revolving door —and Fran, a serious looking woman in her mid-forties with frizzy brown hair tied back with a scrunchie. Emily was glad Fran was working. If there were anything to know about Miles Pemberton, Fran would know it. Not only that, she was very forthcoming with information, at least with Emily and Arabella. She refused to share information with Kerri St. Amour, who, as Truth Seeker, had written an unflattering review of the service at the Sunrise Café. "Didn't get a free meal, was what that was about," Fran had fumed at the time.

She sashayed over to Emily's table, notepad and pen in hand. "What'll it be?"

"Two eggs over easy, home fries, brown toast and coffee, black and strong. No bacon, but I'll take a rasher of gossip if you've got a minute."

A broad smile lit up Fran's plain features. "Coming right up."

🖎

FRAN TOOK the seat opposite Emily after she'd eaten. "Taking my break, new girl will cover the tables."

"New girl? She doesn't have a name?"

"I stop trying to remember them until they've been here a month. So, what can I do for you? Does this have anything with the Hadley house? I hear you and Luke want to put in an offer."

"We're hoping to, but we're up against Miles Pemberton."

"*House Haunters*," Fran said, nodding. "I read about that, not saying where."

Emily stifled a grin. When it came to giving gossip, Fran may have boycotted Kerri, but she wasn't above reading *Outside the Landing*."

"Any scoop on that, beyond what you read?"

"Everyone in town is talking about it, naturally, but no one knows anything."

That was disappointing. "Has Pemberton been in here recently?"

"A few times, always with another guy, silver hair, mid-fifties, suit and tie type. Looks a bit like that guy on *Mad Men*, the one that played Roger Sterling."

"That would be his realtor, Jay Mulacki."

"I've heard his commercials on talk radio. 'Buying or selling? Don't trust any old lackey, hire Jay Mulacki.' Catchy, but I thought Pemberton was viewing properties with Poppy? They were in here together quite a few times last summer. Poppy always picked up the tab. Come to think of it, Mulacki always picks up the tab, too."

That fit in with what Emily had learned about Pemberton. He

used people *and* expected them to pay. "Did you pick up on any of their conversations?"

"That would be eavesdropping."

"I'm sorry, I didn't mean to imply—"

"I did happen to overhear something that might be of interest, though," Fran said, and leaned forward, her voice dropping to a whisper. "When I was setting tables for the lunch crowd, you know, not deliberately listening in."

"Of course."

"The financial backing for *House Haunters* is contingent on the Hadley house having a reputation of being haunted. Those were his exact words. *Contingent on*." Fran sniffed. "Pemberton didn't seem to think it would be a problem, though. He said the townsfolk would fall all over themselves to get on television for their fifteen minutes of fame. Seemed quite smug about it."

Emily's heart sank. "What do you think, Fran? Is he right?"

"He might have been, if he hadn't been going up against you and Luke." Fran patted Emily's hand. "Don't you worry, hon. Here in the Landing, we take care of our own. And everyone wants you two lovebirds to get that house."

38

Emily felt a first hint of optimism, left the Sunrise Café and headed to her next destination, the office of *Inside the Landing* and her arch nemesis, Kerri St. Amour. Unlike the pleasant chat with Fran, however, she had no illusions that this particular visit would be welcome by either of them.

Her phone pinged a few minutes out. Megan.

"Hey."

"I called Faye. We're going to have lunch later." Megan sounded happy.

"I'm glad. Whatever else happens, I hope you two find your way to becoming sisters."

"Sisters. I like the sound of that. Hopefully she feels the same way, though I expect it will take both of us some time to get there, her more than me. But there's something else I thought you'd want to know. When I called, Faye was just wrapping up a meeting with Arabella and Levon. The appraisal is completed and whatever the mysterious document was, it's now off the table. The house is officially going back on the market."

"That's great," Emily said, though in truth she'd hoped for a couple of days delay. Would there be enough time to implement Operation: Takedown Miles Pemberton?

"I suggested extending offer day to Wednesday, allowing for the time the house was off the market. Faye sounded surprised, but amenable. I think she had the same idea."

"Thank you."

"Sisters in solidarity," Megan said.

Emily had no sooner disconnected than her phone pinged again. This time it was Sydney.

"I was able to reach about a dozen people who have been burned by Miles Pemberton," Sydney said, getting straight to the point. "The good news is that eight of them are willing to speak out about their experience. The bad news is no one will do so unless it's done anonymously. Four are too frightened to take a stand. I didn't want to push them. If Pemberton finds out, his revenge will be fast and furious."

"Eight is better than we expected and anonymous shouldn't be a problem. Can you email me the list of names and their contact information?"

"Will do. I'll let them know you'll be in touch."

"I appreciate that. I'm just about at Kerri's office now. I'll call you later, let you know what's happening."

"There's one more thing you should know before you meet with her," Sydney said, "and you'll never guess what it is."

❧

THE OFFICE of *Inside the Landing* was housed inside a converted rooming house that had seen better days even when Emily had been the paper's editor, and not much had changed. The landlord and owner of Print It! still occupied the largest space in the building. The other tenants included a computer repair shop, and a husband and wife team who sold mail-order merchandise, mostly crap, as Emily remembered.

She rang the doorbell to Suite 3 and waited, her nerves,

hangover, and greasy breakfast playing havoc with her head and stomach. *What the heck had she been thinking?*

Kerri St. Amour opened the door. A tall, reed-thin brunette with a long, slender neck and warm brown eyes, she reminded Emily of Audrey Hepburn in *My Fair Lady*. The visual didn't make Emily feel any better. She loved old musicals, and it was one of her favorites.

A look of surprise, then curiosity, crossed Kerri's face before being replaced by one of annoyance. "Emily Garland. To what do I owe the displeasure?"

Emily swallowed. "I have a proposition for you."

A door down the hall squeaked open.

"You better come in," Kerri said. "The halls and walls have big ears."

The interior space wasn't much larger than a decent-sized bedroom, containing a corner workspace and two chairs, but Kerri had managed to put her own stamp on it: lavender walls filled with paintings of spring flowers—lilacs, hyacinth, daffodils, tulips, cherry blossoms, and lilies—all dated and signed KSA.

"Your work?" Emily asked.

"Yes."

"They're beautiful. Truly."

"Thank you. I should probably branch out to something beyond flowers, but they bring me peace. But you're not here to discuss my artistic pursuits. You said you had a proposition. I can't imagine what you could offer that would be of interest to the readers of *Inside the Landing*. We don't run advertorials."

The last sentence was meant to sting, Emily knew. During her brief tenure, she'd entertained the idea of advertorials, not that she'd lasted long enough to implement them. She ignored the barb.

"This isn't about the newspaper. It's about *Outside the Landing* and your alter ego, Truth Seeker."

"You think I'm Truth Seeker?" she asked with a smirk.

"Let's not play games. You and I both know you've used that platform to cast aspersions on Arabella, the Glass Dolphin, Levon, and me. And I get it. You and I have a history, one that goes back to before either of us had even heard of Lount's Landing. I'm asking you to put that aside."

"And why would I do that?"

"Because our feud goes back to our earliest days as freelancers for *Urban Living*. We were pitted against one another from day one, by individuals ruthless enough not to care. And ever since, the powers-that-be have been fueling that fire for their personal gain, not ours."

"Maybe you haven't gained anything, but I certainly have. In case you've forgotten, I'm the editor now."

"You accepted the job of editor for *Inside the Landing* when you were positioned to move up the corporate ladder at Urban Huntzberger. Your vision never involved moving to a small town to take over a local paper, you know that as well as I do. They used you to quash me, because I'd gotten too close to a story they didn't want told."

"Your point would be?"

Time to reveal Sydney's "one more thing."

"I know you applied for the position of publicity director at CKHTV. You were one of the top contenders, but Miles Pemberton made sure you wouldn't be hired. I don't know what you did to get on the wrong side of him, but whatever it was, your chances at a job at CKHTV are slim and none. Unless…" Emily let the sentence dangle.

Hook.

"Unless what?"

Line.

"I have a plan that involves Truth Seeker. A plan that might reopen the door for you at CKHTV."

"I'm listening."

And sinker.

39

———

Pemberton had been unimpressed with Truth Seeker's recap of the dollar store incident. "He said I hadn't been harsh enough on you and demanded that I write another post. I refused." Kerri flushed. "My posts may be filled with gossip and innuendo, but I'm still a journalist, and I draw the line at writing an outright lie. After the blog ran, I heard from a couple of people who'd been at the store that day. They defended you, said Pemberton had acted like a class-A jerk. I told him that if I wrote another post, it would include their feedback. He told me I'd live to regret my decision. I went from having a second round of interviews at CKHTV to—two days later —a form letter rejection."

Emily wasn't so sure that Kerri's idea of innuendo versus outright lies coincided with hers, but she wasn't about to question it, especially now. "That feedback would have vindicated me. You would have done that?"

Kerri rolled her eyes. "Don't be ridiculous. But Pemberton didn't know that, and I don't appreciate being bullied."

Emily got the double meaning. "I'm not here to bully you, Kerri. I'm here because I think we can help each other."

Kerri nodded. "All right, as long as you don't expect me to get all Kumbaya around the campfire with you."

"Deal."

Once she was on board, Kerri was all in. "What I can do," she told Emily, "is schedule one or more blog posts on *Outside the Landing*. How many people that worked with Pemberton are willing to come forward with their story?"

"Eight, so far, though others may come forward if they feel secure enough to do so. However, all eight individuals have insisted on being quoted as an anonymous source. My plan was to call them for their stories, write them up, and email them to you without any names attached."

Kerri's lips thinned to a single line. "Without names attached? If this is going to work, we have to trust one another."

"It's not about a lack of trust," Emily said, even though it was partly that. "It's because should Pemberton, or anyone for that matter, decide to confront you, you can quite honestly say that while you trust your source implicitly, you are unaware of the individuals' identities."

"What if he asks who my source is? How do you know I won't throw you under the bus?"

"I don't." Emily forced a smile. "I guess that's where the mutual trust comes in."

"When do we start?"

"I'll start phoning folks as soon as I get home. With luck, I'll have all eight interviews to you by the end of day."

"What about timing? Were you thinking one a day?"

Emily thought about that. Eight days, starting tomorrow, would take them through to next Saturday. Offer day for the Hadley house was on Wednesday. "I was hoping to be more aggressive than that."

"Aggressive is my specialty." Kerri grinned. "Pemberton is about to find out that hell hath no fury like two women scorned."

Emily laughed. "Make that four women and counting."

40

THE FIRST POST on *Outside the Landing* was up at seven a.m. Sunday morning. Emily didn't know what she'd been expecting, but it wasn't this.

Seeker continues to seek out the Real Truth.

Emily clicked off, tears threatening to spill down her cheeks. Kerri had laid the groundwork for Operation: Takedown Miles Pemberton, and she'd done it by coming to her defense.

☛

Arabella phoned an hour later. "Did you see today's *Outside the Landing?*"

"Uh huh. It was an unexpected surprise, but at least this time it was a pleasant one."

"Hmm. Well, I don't trust her."

"Perhaps Kerri has decided to take the high road from now on."

"Look at you, all forgive and forget."

"I'm just saying, people can change."

"People, yes. People like Kerri St. Amour? No. At least that's what you've always led me to believe. So, what's going on? What aren't you telling me?"

Emily could have said nothing was going on, but she'd never lied to Arabella in the past, and she wasn't about to start now. She began with her visit to Sydney and their evening of drinks at the Noose with Megan Sutcliffe.

"So that's why Sydney came back to town," Arabella said when she'd finished. "Poor kid. Miles Pemberton doesn't sound like a very nice guy. It does explain Faye's request, though. She called me last night, asked if Levon and I would meet with Megan to go over our appraisal of the Hadley house in detail. I thought it was an exercise in self-protection, what with the bad blood between them. But from what you've told me, maybe they're trying to work together and put their differences aside."

"I hope so. Grudges fester inside us, and for what?"

"Ah-ha," Arabella said. "And that brings us right back to Kerri St. Amour."

"Actually, it brings us to Operation: Takedown Miles Pemberton," Emily said, and laid out the plan.

41

Emily laughed out loud at the headline.

No Smiles Working With Miles
    Miles Pemberton may charm fans of Pemberton on Property with his good looks and easy smile, but those who work with him at CKHTV say he's two-faced, one side for the public, quite another in private.

What followed was a string of one-liners from anonymous sources. Emily had to admire Kerri's style. She'd managed to take the interviews and dig out a dozen quotes. Anyone reading it would assume twelve individuals had stepped forward, versus the eight Sydney had lined up. And yet, not a single quote had been embellished, nor did it have to be. The one thing Emily had learned during her multiple conversations yesterday was that Miles was almost universally disliked. The last paragraph packed a punch.

Sounds like it's Pemberton's way or the highway, a one-way street where anyone who dares to go in another direction will find themselves looking for a new job in another industry. And that might mean you too, Mr. Pemberton. We hear the network's pockets weren't deep enough for you. Word of warning: What goes around, comes around. In fact, this blogger is going to make sure of it.

It didn't take long for the post to go viral, be shared repeatedly on social media, and, as Sydney had predicted, more people had come forward with their own stories. By the time Monday's morning post had gone out with more claims of Pemberton's abuse of power and privilege, *Outside the Landing's* subscriber list had quadrupled, and according to Kerri, the numbers were growing by the minute.

It had also captured the attention of the CKHTV executives, thanks to Dwight Sutcliffe. "They promised my father they'd do a thorough inquiry," Megan told Emily. "As I understand it just being an ass won't get you fired. But Pemberton has been part of a string of iffy business deals, his advertisers are backing out, and the network's legal department is nervous. They pulled *House Haunters, Pemberton on Property* has been put on hiatus, and Pemberton has been ordered to take an unpaid sabbatical. He was denying all accusations, but the last day or so he's been quiet. Maybe his attorney—or the network—told him to shut up."

Emily thought about Sydney. "Kerri was right. What goes around really does come around."

"Yeah. Karma, you gotta love it. The network might bring back *House Haunters* with a new host. It's still a solid program idea. I can only imagine what Pemberton would think of that. My guess is *P on P* will be cancelled. Pemberton will drop out of sight, at least for a whil. He's been humiliated in the public eye, and it would take quite a spin-doctor to make that go away. There might be years of legal suits, and who knows? After a few years he might try to sell another idea to the network."

Emily hadn't thought about the possibility of a lawsuit. Arabella would flip. Never mind Arabella. Luke would flip. "Do you think Pemberton will sue me or Kerri or any of us?"

"My father assures me that won't happen, and he's seldom wrong. His money and his army of lawyers can be quite persuasive."

And then the implications of everything that Megan had told her hit Emily full force. "That means the Hadley house—"

"Is one step closer to being yours."

42

———————

TUESDAY MORNING'S headline in *Outside the Landing* said it all: *PEMBERTON SENT PACKING*. Emily was just about to read it when her phone buzzed. Kerri. But she'd already talked to Sydney and Kerri last night, the three of them feeling victorious, plans for a repeat girl's night out at the Noose already underway, this time with Arabella included.

Could something have gone wrong? Could Pemberton be threatening legal action, despite Megan's assurances to the contrary? Emily's stomach roiled.

"What's up?"

"I just heard from an inside source at RECO, the Real Estate Council of Ontario. According to my source, who shall remain nameless, Bob Wilkes has just filed an ethics complaint against Jay Mulacki."

Emily searched her memory. Poppy had said Wilkes had agent's remorse over getting mixed up with Mulacki and Pemberton, though at the time she didn't know why. "What's the complaint?"

"Rumor has it the Hadley house was over the network's budget and Pemberton asked Mulacki to 'loan' him money for the down payment. There are laws against this—and we don't know if any money passed hands. We do know Mulacki was double-ending a deal and didn't present an offer written up by Wilkes."

"What does 'double ending' mean?"

"It means the agent was representing the buyer and the seller. Beyond that, I suggest you call Poppy Spencer. Word is she's getting tight again with Wilkes."

Poppy was reluctant at first, but once Emily told her she was aware of the RECO complaint against Mulacki, she was more than willing to talk, even if it was only in hypothetical terms.

"Let's say Broker A lists a property for the Seller."

"Okay."

"Three days after the property is listed, Broker B calls Broker A and tells him he'll be coming in with an offer. Broker A acknowledges the conversation, and shortly thereafter, Broker B submits his clients' offer. So far, so good, right?"

"Right," Emily said.

"Except it's not. A week later, the house comes up as sold. And it's twenty grand under the amount offered by Broker B's clients. Now, when it comes to dealings with Broker A, this sort of thing has happened to Broker B before, but the dollar difference has always been negligible, two or three thousand dollars. And so, the deal seemed legit. The offer might have had an extra bonus, or one less condition, something like that. Are you with me so far?"

"Yes."

"But this time," Poppy said, "a lot more money is at stake. And that makes Broker B suspicious. So one day, knowing he might even be risking sanctions, he knocks on the door of the Seller and asks why they took the offer for $20k less. And guess what he found out?"

"I don't know," Emily said.

"That they only had the one offer. The offer from Broker A's client." Poppy paused for effect. "In other words, Broker A never presented Broker B's offer. And so Broker B asks the Seller if they'd be willing to write a statement to that effect. And they do. In fact, they're in the process of suing Broker A. I believe the folks that lost out on the house are also considering legal action."

"Wow."

"Yeah, wow."

"What will happen to Broker A?"

"RECO will do a thorough investigation. If the charges are substantiated, there will, at the very least, be a substantial financial penalty. There's a strong likelihood that Broker A's license will be suspended or revoked."

"And in the interim?"

"Broker A can continue to operate, business as usual."

"I guess it's just as well that Pemberton's out, then."

"You can say that again," Poppy said. "And before you consider sharing anything with me on how that transpired, think again. There are some things I'd rather not know."

⟜

ARABELLA CALLED EMILY IMMEDIATELY after reading the post on *Outside the Landing*. She was glad that Pemberton was out, but, the appraisal now behind her, she'd finally had time to seriously consider co-owning 21 Walnut Street. As much as she wanted to help Emily and Luke, and as much as she'd always admired the house, the more she thought about it, the worse the idea seemed. They were business partners and best friends. Going through the process of obtaining permits, the actual renovation—who would pay for what, would they agree on contractors, and eventually living next door to one another—was bound to put a strain on one or both relationships.

Emily answered on the first ring. After the usual pleasantries and a quick recap on how everything had unfolded, Arabella got straight to the point.

"I can't do it, Emily. Go in on the Hadley house with you and Luke. It's not just the money, it's—"

"I know. It's our friendship. The business. To be honest, Luke wasn't on board from the beginning." Emily didn't mention that he'd suggested selling all or part of her fifty percent share in the Glass Dolphin. Things were tough enough at the shop with both of them sharing the hours and the expenses. She couldn't put Arabella in that position. "Luke's been crunching the numbers and he thinks the cost to convert the house back to the duplex will be prohibitive. And that's if we can get the building permits. I was going to call you later today."

Arabella gave a silent sigh of relief. "Great minds think alike. When do you meet with Poppy to prepare your offer?"

"Two p.m. tomorrow. But even with Pemberton out, Poppy thinks we'll still be in competition. There's been a lot of interest in the house, ironically much of it generated by *Outside the Landing*."

"Nothing like a little notoriety to garner attention."

"Yeah." Emily sighed. "Unfortunately, we can't afford to go in much over asking."

"I might have an idea," Arabella said. "Let me make a phone call first. I'll get back to you before you meet with Poppy tomorrow."

43

———

Arabella called Emily first thing Wednesday morning. "I might have a solution," she said, "but I'm not sure how you're going to feel about it."

"I'm open to any reasonable suggestion." Emily gave a nervous laugh. "I might even entertain an unreasonable suggestion. I barely slept last night."

"I'm not sure what category this falls under, but here goes. As you know, Caitie Meadows fills in for each of us whenever we need her."

"Uh huh."

"About a month ago, Caitie mentioned that she'd like to expand her jewelry business beyond consignment and online sales. She discussed brick-and-mortar options with Poppy and talked to an accountant, but the idea of going full-on storefront solo intimidates the heck out of her. She also really enjoys working at the Glass Dolphin. So she wondered if there was a way to combine the two."

"Are you suggesting what I think you're suggesting? That we offer Caitie an option to buy into the Glass Dolphin?"

"That's exactly what I'm suggesting, and before you say no, she's not looking to be a full partner. Rather, she'd be interested in buying half of your share in the Glass Dolphin. It would mean that I would retain fifty percent, and you'd each own twenty-five. Another option is that we'd each own one-third. Equal partners all the way…" Arabella's voice trailed off into the deafening silence on the other end. She'd gone too far, overstepped the boundaries. "Emily? Are you still there?"

"Yes," she said with a loud sniff.

"Are you crying?"

"I still have a cold," Emily said.

"So you're not crying?"

"Oh, yeah, I'm crying, because I can't believe what a great friend you are."

"So you're not mad at me?"

"Mad? Quite the opposite. Luke suggested selling, and not just because of the money. We're hoping to have a baby as soon as we can, and then I'll want to take some time off and, well, I just didn't know how to tell you, and I didn't want to hurt your feel—"

"Enough ands," Arabella said, laughing. "I guess the only questions are do we go halves or thirds?"

"It was your store before I came on board, and in my mind, it will always be your store. Whatever you want, Arabella."

Arabella had spent a long night thinking about it. Like Emily, she had a plan for the future, or at least, the beginnings of a plan. "In that case, I'll take thirty-four percent. I promise not to lord the extra percentage over you and Caitie."

"Ha. As if we'd let you get away with that. But even with Caitie's cash, it probably won't come up to much."

"We're debt free, have a decent amount of inventory, and we've established goodwill, but you're right, it's going to be a far cry from massive. We'll also need to find an appraiser, hire a lawyer to draft up the contract, and meet with the bank. Or maybe the bank is the first step. I'll get the ball rolling today." Arabella paused. "It may not happen fast enough to help you with the house, though."

"Whatever happens, I want you to know I appreciate you looking out for me. You're the best friend I've ever had."

"Don't be getting all sentimental on me. Now hang up and go buy a house."

But it was Arabella getting sentimental once they'd disconnected. It wouldn't be long and Emily would be on maternity leave. Maybe she'd bring the baby into the store, let Auntie Arabella teach him or her that authenticity mattered. The thought made her happy.

Poppy walked Emily and Luke through the paperwork. "I spoke to Bob. He's expecting four other offers."

"Four," Emily said, her heart sinking. Luke took her hand and squeezed it.

"Four," Poppy repeated. "Which means we need to go in without conditions."

"I can forgo the home inspection," Luke said. "I've already inspected it top to bottom. But we need ten days to sort out additional financing. Right now, we've only been pre-approved to go in at five thousand dollars over asking."

Poppy shook her head. "I wouldn't recommend adding a ten-day finance condition. In my experience, the cleanest offer usually wins. The way the vendor is going to look at it is that there's no guarantee you'll come up with the financing, and then they'll be back to entertaining offers. Go in firm, no conditions, with your best and final offer. I'll present that way so there's not a lot of unnecessary back and forth. Okay?"

Emily and Luke nodded, signing on the many dotted lines.

"I'll let you know as soon as I hear anything, but I expect it will be several hours," Poppy said. "The offers aren't being presented until five. You two grab something to eat and then go for a walk or something."

EMILY HAD RUN the Toronto Waterfront Marathon, all twenty-six point two miles of it, but she was pretty sure that her and Luke walked that much and more as they waited to hear from Poppy. Nervous, but knowing it was the right thing to do, she'd filled him in on Operation: Takedown Miles Pemberton, but instead of being angry with her, he'd only laughed, saying he better not get on the wrong side of her or any of her friends.

After that, Luke told her about the Snowmobile, ATV & Powersports Show—exhausting, but worthwhile, with decent sales and lots of networking— and his idea for a summer regatta hosted by the marina. That led to talk of the Glass Dolphin, and the proposed partnership with Caitie, and everything else that had been going on the past few days, and more walking and talking.

But as the town's clock struck six, Emily couldn't stand it any longer. "Let's go by the house. I have to see it. See who's there."

"Me, too," Luke said.

They walked hand in hand to Walnut Street, past the cars lined up in the driveway at number 21. There were eight of them, including Poppy's white Mercedes. *Were there eight offers?* Emily wondered. No, that wouldn't make sense. Faye Everett would have to be there, and maybe Megan, someone from the bank.

They kept walking, winding their way down the tree-lined street, silent now as they admired the Victorian architecture, every house different from the one next to it.

And then they saw it. A miniature version of the Hadley house, a realtor's sign in the front bay window.

COMING SOON.

Emily's phone chimed at that very moment. Poppy. An omen?

"I'm so sorry," Poppy said. "I fought for you but you didn't get it."

"It's okay," Emily said, and this time she squeezed Luke's hand. "I think we just found our dream home."

44

———

One ninety-four Walnut Street officially came on the market two weeks later. This time there was no duplex option, making it considerably more affordable. Even better, during the Coming Soon phase, the owners had made a few improvements, including a new roof, furnace, and air conditioner, and fresh paint throughout. Not a hint of wallpaper, flowery or otherwise.

Thanks to Poppy, Emily and Luke wasted no time putting in their best offer, and this time their pre-approved mortgage was more than enough to succeed.

The process of her and Arabella splitting their ownership shares in the Glass Dolphin went ahead, Caitie as excited as a kid at Christmas, Emily and Arabella feeling positive about the change.

But as the old saying goes, everything happens in threes.

The news was announced in *Inside the Landing* a month later.

Garland Back as St. Amour Makes Tracks
   By Kerri St. Amour

It's been a wonderful four-and-a-half years as Editor of INSIDE THE LANDING, *but this reporter has received an offer she can't refuse. Effective immediately, I will be stepping down to assume the position of publicity director at CKHTV.*

My temporary replacement, acting as interim managing editor, will be Emily Garland, a longtime journalist, well-known to the residents of Lount's Landing. Garland will be implementing an exciting new program that starts with recruiting four interns from the journalism program at Cedar County College in Lakeside. Under her direction, each intern will learn the ins and outs of running a local newspaper, from editorial to advertising (trust me, in this job, one size fits all). The best candidate will earn the job of editor. Thank you, Ms. Garland, for stepping up during this transition period.

Emily smiled. Kerri had made it clear she owed her, and this was her payback. She was going to be busy, but she didn't mind. Now that there were three of them on shift for the shop, she had the time, and it would be fun mentoring the students. The bit of extra money wouldn't hurt either, what with the new house and the wedding, and hopefully, a baby. She kept reading, knowing that Kerri had saved the best news for last.

My first official announcement as publicity director is to welcome Sydney Van Fraassen to the CKHTV team. Most of you will be familiar with Sydney's Smoothie Shop on Main Street and never fear: the shop will remain, with a new owner, Gloria Moroziuk. Readers might remember Gloria as the former owner of the Sunrise Café. Seems she missed living in the Landing. We missed you too, Gloria! As for Ms. Van Fraassen, she'll be an executive producer on two new television series: REALITY RV: LIVE FREE AND DRIVE *and* OPENING UP SHOP. *Congratulations, Sydney!*

What Kerri hadn't announced, because it wasn't local news, was the official cancellation of *Pemberton on Property*. According to Megan, Pemberton was all but finished in the reality television arena. She'd been especially pleased to learn that Megan and Faye had moved towards the next rung of reconciliation: working together on a new show, tentatively titled *Newlywed Wish List*. Emily had respectively declined the offer to be interviewed.

She and Arabella had also put the offer of a documentary on daguerreotypes on the back burner. For the time being, they'd both had enough of reality TV to last a lifetime. But they hadn't closed the door. Not completely.

Never say never, right?

The next day, Truth Seeker posted that *Outside the Landing* was on permanent hiatus. No one who followed the blog was surprised; everyone knew Kerri St. Amour was Truth Seeker. And, in true small town fashion, even those who didn't pretended that they did.

45

———

Arabella placed the diamond pendant around Emily's neck, remembering the first time the two of them had met. She'd arrived at the Glass Dolphin a week before the grand opening, and found a slender woman in a thin coat shivering by the front door. Arabella had made similar wardrobe miscalculations in November, a month where the prevailing Lount's Landing winds could be as unpredictable as an eBay auction.

That had been five years ago. It turned out she and Emily had plenty in common, including a penchant for getting involved in things that weren't necessarily their business, including murder. Solving them, that is, not committing them. And now here she was, Emily's matron of honor—or was that maid? She finished fastening the clasp of the "something borrowed" necklace. The diamond solitaire had originally been a gift from Levon on her own wedding day a dozen years earlier. She'd wondered if it might be bad luck, since she and Levon were no longer together, but Emily had just laughed and said that nothing was ever going to come between her and Luke. Arabella hoped with her whole heart that was true.

She surveyed Emily now, a lump forming in her throat. All brides were beautiful, but to her eyes, Emily had eclipsed beautiful, her long, dark hair swept in an updo, diamond studs sparkling in her ears. She'd wanted a winter wedding, and her dress was perfect—white velvet, the bodice embellished with Swarovski crystals, the bottom long, loose, and free flowing.

"You look incredible," Arabella said. "Luke is one lucky guy."

"We're both lucky. He's my soul mate, you know?"

Soul mate, Arabella thought, and nodded. For the first time that day, she felt sad. She pushed the feeling aside and smoothed the imaginary wrinkles of her own dress, a replica of Emily's in midnight blue velvet, albeit with fewer crystals. The first time she'd tried it on—she'd been wearing Levon's diamond pendant—she felt like a princess. She choked back the emotion. This was Emily and Luke's day, not hers.

"It's time," Arabella said. "Mustn't keep Luke waiting."

LUKE STOOD SOLDIER-STRAIGHT at the front of the chapel, handsome in his black suit and white velvet cummerbund, his dark eyes misting at the sight of Emily. His best man, Hudson Tanaka, stood by his side, his posture equally rigid. Like Luke, he wore a black suit, with a midnight blue cummerbund to match Arabella's dress.

With the exception of a Jack and Jill shower, she hadn't seen Hudson since they'd broken up a few months back. It had been an amicable split, and she'd enjoyed his company. He was both interesting and intelligent, not to mention easy on the eyes. But good looks didn't pave the road for a lasting relationship, and they both knew they'd never last.

And so, Arabella had been genuinely happy for him upon learning that his Medieval Knight book series had been optioned for television. Unfortunately, he had one fatal flaw.

He wasn't Levon.

46

THE WEDDING RECEPTION was held at The Hanged Man's Noose, the bar laden with velvety white poinsettias, the tips lightly dusted with midnight blue and crystal clear glitter. In addition to a bottle of white and red wines, every table held a pitcher of Treasontinis. Betsy had outdone herself, frosting blueberries so they shimmered like stars in the pub's intimate lighting.

Emily thought back to the first time she'd met Betsy Ehrlich; the morning of the Glass Dolphin's grand opening and Betsy had stopped by with appetizers and bite-sized desserts. She remembered thinking that pubs weren't her thing, despite Arabella's enthusiastic endorsement of the Noose's food and nineteenth century saloon decor, and her assurance that it wasn't a pickup joint like you found in the city.

Arabella had been right, and Emily had since shared many enjoyable hours here with Arabella, Levon, and more recently, Hudson and Luke. When it came to selecting a venue for their reception, she hadn't even considered going anywhere else. Betsy had become family.

Family. She still missed her parents every single day, wished a thousand times they could have met Luke, could have been here to celebrate and share in her happiness. But Luke's parents were there, a lovely couple who truly seemed to embrace her. She glanced around the room until her gaze landed on her husband, her heart overflowing with love and pride as he mingled effortlessly with their guests.

She couldn't wait for Luke to carry her over the threshold of their new house so they could begin their life together. But right now, there was a party going on, and she was determined to enjoy every last minute of it.

THE BUFFET DINNER had been served with accolades from all factions. Betsy had ensured that everyone, from ardent vegan to unapologetic meat lover, was equally satiated—and the speeches, heartfelt but blessedly short, were over. Now, as the tables and chairs were being moved to make room for a temporary dance floor, Arabella took the opportunity to slip into the shadowy corners of the pub and people watch.

There were a handful of folks Arabella didn't recognize, almost certainly friends of Emily and Luke's, her impression confirmed by the way they hung out together, hovering around the head table. It made Arabella all the more aware of how well Emily had integrated into the community.

The DJ began playing Blue Rodeo's *Lost Together*, a cue for Luke and Emily to take center stage for their first dance before inviting others to join in. Arabella pushed back a tear, watched the dance floor fill up, and contemplated the pairings.

Stanford McLelland and Michelle Ellis. Arabella had been surprised when Stanford had asked if he could bring Emily's ex-employer as his plus one, and even more surprised when Emily said yes. "Without Michelle, I'd never have moved to Lount's Landing," she'd explained, and while Arabella conceded she had a point, she couldn't imagine having that much forgiveness in her heart.

On the other side of the room, a young man Arabella recognized as the latest owner of Frankie's Fish & Chips was flirting shamelessly with Sydney Van Fraassen, who was flirting right back. *Who's the smoothie operator* now, she thought, grinning at her very bad pun.

Seated at the table next to Sydney was Nigel Watters, owner of the Sunrise Café, and the diner's waitress, Fran, her uniform replaced by a sleek burgundy sheath, her usually frizzy hair slicked into submission. Were they were friends or something more? They certainly appeared to be sharing an intimate moment.

Caitie Meadows, looking radiant in red, was laughing and dancing with a cousin of Luke's. From the looks on their faces, it wouldn't be their last dance. Nor did it look like it would be the last dance for Betsy and Robbie Andrews, the head pro at the Miakoda Falls Golf and Country Club. When did that happen? Arabella didn't even know that Betsy golfed.

Was that Poppy Spencer dancing with Bob Wilkes? Emily had said their decades-old feud had been laid to rest following the Hadley house business. It seemed forgiveness was all around her.

Forgiveness. Maybe it was finally time. Her gaze landed on Levon, sitting alone at the bar and looking too handsome for his own good. Who was she kidding? For *her* own good. She took a deep breath and walked over to the bar, sliding into the empty seat next to him.

"Courvoisier," she told the bartender.

Levon turned to face her and smiled, the full-on one that always melted her heart. "You look beautiful, Bella. Blue velvet becomes you."

"You clean up nice, too." She downed the cognac, feeling the burn go down her throat and deep into her belly. She stood up. "I have to get some fresh air."

"I'll get your wrap and come out with you, if that's okay."

Arabella wished she'd ordered a double. Wished she could say, "No, thanks, I'd rather be alone." Instead she found herself saying, "That would be nice."

Levon and Arabella stood side-by-side at the lamppost outside The Hanged Man's Noose. The air was cold and crisp, the stars bright against the inky night sky. Arabella shivered, knowing it had nothing to do with the temperature.

"Are you cold?" Levon asked, his voice filled with concern. "If so, we should head back inside."

"No. Yes. I mean, I'm a little bit cold but. .I have to say something first." *While I have the nerve,* she thought, knowing it was now or never. No more half measures.

"Sounds serious," Levon said.

"Yeah, it is."

"I'm here for you."

Arabella resisted the urge to hug him. *Not yet,* she told herself. *Not yet.* "You've always been there for me, Levon. No matter what we've gone through, I've never doubted that, not for a moment. Which is why I was wondering if you might consider…" Her voice trailed off and for a moment she wondered if she could go through with it. And then Levon spoke, his voice soft and husky.

"Consider?"

Arabella took a deep breath. She could do this.

"I wondered if…if you'd like to…to marry me again."

Levon pulled a green velvet ring box out of his coat pocket.

"I thought you'd never ask."

THE END

AUTHOR'S NOTE

The inspiration for the Glass Dolphin antiques shop came from an assignment in *The Words Wanting Out,* a creative writing workshop led by Barry Dempster, an award winning author and poet, who also became a friend and mentor. It was early days in my fiction writing life, somewhere around 2010, and the assignment was to write a short mystery story that included the words Blue and Dolphin.

I was the Senior Editor for (the now defunct) *New England Antiques Journal* at the time, and so I started writing a story about an antiques shop called the Blue Dolphin. For no reason that I can remember, the name Arabella popped into my head. I don't think I'd ever heard the name before (although I have since…it's sort of like when you drive a white Honda Civic…all of a sudden, all the cars you see are white Honda Civics). The Carpenter? I was listening to the radio and *Close to You,* an old song by The Carpenters, came on. Arabella Carpenter, I thought. That has a nice ring to it.

Also, at the time, I was living in Holland Landing, a small town about ninety minutes north of Toronto, where the most infamous resident is Samuel Lount, a politician and pacifist who was hanged for treason in the nineteenth century. And so, Lount's Landing was born, albeit with nearby Newmarket's Main Street of independent shops and businesses.

I'd like to tell you the short story was a winner, but in truth, it was quite dreadful. But I liked the irascible Arabella Carpenter, for whom "authenticity mattered," and I loved my setting. In 2012, after attending Bloody Words, a mystery writing conference in Toronto, I decided to take the premise of the story and write a novel (ignorance truly is bliss).

While Arabella and Lount's Landing stuck, I changed the name of the shop to the Glass Dolphin after I found out there was a real life Blue Dolphin antiques shop in Maine. Next, I created Emily Garland, a Toronto-based freelance journalist who takes on a lucrative undercover assignment in Lount's Landing with her own hidden agenda. I'd been a freelance journalist and editor since 2003, specializing in antiques and the residential housing industry, and so I knew the world she was coming from (not that I was ever offered a lucrative undercover assignment). I always knew that I'd have an Emily in my first book—the book that motivated me to be a writer as far back as a child was *Emily Climbs* by L.M. Montgomery. As for the Garland, we have my mother to thank for that, as her favorite actress and singer was the legendary Judy Garland.

The character of Levon Larroquette—Levon after the Elton John song and Larroquette after the actor, John—was the most fun to write, perhaps because in my head he looks like a young Kris Kristofferson. Not sure what that looks like? Google *A Star is Born*, 1976. Better yet, watch the movie. At any rate, I wanted an on-again-off-again-on-again relationship between Arabella and her ex, and back in my younger days, cognac altered my good judgement more times than I care to admit.

Readers often ask who my favorite character is, and while Emily and I certainly share many things in common, including a love of running, hands down it's Arabella. I love that she wears her heart on her sleeve, that authenticity matters to her, that she's a bit feisty, unfailingly optimistic, loyal to a fault, but nobody's fool. It's also the reason I've included Arabella as a minor character in my Marketville Mystery series.

The Hanged Man's Noose, book #1 in the Glass Dolphin Mystery series, was first contracted in July 2014 and published in July 2015 by Barking Rain Press. I will be forever grateful to Sheri Gormley, the publisher at BRP, for believing in me, and my story.

When I set about writing book #3, *Where There's a Will*, I knew it would be the final book in the series. I have so many stories living inside my head, the words wanting out, and time is a non-renewable commodity. But I also knew that I had to leave Arabella, Emily, and Levon at a good place in their lives. I think I've done that. I hope you do, too.

Judy Penz Sheluk
    November 2020

ACKNOWLEDGMENTS

Writing may be a solitary process, but researching the facts behind the fiction takes a village. My heartfelt thanks to the following individuals; any mistakes are mine alone:

My nephew, Brian Sametz. A longtime real estate professional, Brian's recounting of a real-life, double-ended deal took the story in a direction I hadn't expected. I love when that happens.

Carole McGill Plant, realtor and friend, for her tutorial on RECO, brokerage rules, and bully offers.

Daniel Fiorini, for his expertise in estate law, holograph wills, the phrase "you can't reach out from the grave," and his tireless efforts to answer my questions without charging a single billable hour.

John Fiske, for his article on Witch Bottles in his excellent online publication, *Digital Antiques Journal*. You can find the article here: https://antiquesjournal.com/index.php/2018/12/14/yours-sincerely-witch-bottles/

I would also be remiss if I didn't acknowledge the people behind some of the names:

Robert Wilkes, a great guy whose only stipulation for Bob Wilkes was that he not be a womanizer. Next time, you might want to be more specific, Robert…just saying.

Longtime friends Louise van Fraassen Smith and Paul Smith, with a nod to their RV, the Taj Mah Paul.

My "furniture daughter," Sydney Smith. May you keep on Shifting Forward.

My gratitude also goes to:

Beta readers Kathleen Costa, Michele Malchuk, and beta reader/proofreader Jennifer Grybowski, for your insights and support as I continue this journey.

Ti Locke, for her hawk-eyed editing and thoughtful feedback, and for always being in my corner.

Last, but certainly not least, my husband, Mike, beta reader, believer, and everything in between, the Ricky to my Lucy, the Levon to my Arabella. None of this would have been possible without your love and encouragement.

SKELETONS IN THE ATTIC

A Marketville Mystery #1
Judy Penz Sheluk

Four Chapter Preview

1

———————

I'D BEEN SITTING in the reception area of Hampton & Associates for the better part of an hour when Leith Hampton finally charged in through the main door, his face flushed, a faint scent of sandalwood cologne wafting into the room. He held an overstuffed black briefcase in each hand and muttered an apology about a tough morning in court before barking out a flurry of instructions to a harried-looking associate. A tail-wagging goldendoodle appeared out of nowhere, and I realized the dog had been sleeping under the receptionist's desk.

Leith nodded towards his office, a signal for me to go in and take a seat, then followed me, plopping both briefcases on his desk. He leaned down to pat the dog and pulled a biscuit out of his pants pocket. "Atticus," he said, not looking up. "My personal therapy dog. Some days, he's the only thing that keeps me sane."

I nodded, slipping into a chair closest to the window. It wasn't a particularly large office, and you definitely got some street noise—horns honking, sirens, the occasional revving of a motorcycle engine—but it did offer a decent view of Bay Street. I watched as countless individuals of every possible size, shape, and color scurried along the street, as cyclists—completely insane in my opinion— weaved their way in and out of the endless stream of gridlocked traffic. In the heart of Toronto's financial district, everyone was always in a hurry, even if getting somewhere in a hurry wasn't possible.

Atticus took up residence in a chair by the corner. Going by the blanket that covered the fabric, this was his regular seating arrangement. It amused me to think that Leith Hampton, a criminal defense attorney known for his blistering cross-examinations and ruthless antics, both in and out of court, owned a goldendoodle, let alone one that was allowed on the furniture.

After a good fifteen minutes, a half dozen consultations with more harried-looking associates, and three telephone calls, all brief, Leith was apparently satisfied he'd sorted out what needed to be done and who was going to do it. He looked up at me, and I realized what made people gravitate towards him. It wasn't his five-foot, six-inch frame, mostly slender with the exception of a slight paunch, but his eyes; eyes so blue, so intense in their gaze, that they seemed electric.

He opened a drawer and removed a manila file folder along with a thin document bound in pale blue cardboard, the words LAST WILL AND TESTAMENT OF JAMES DAVID BARNSTABLE etched in black on the cover. "Let's go into the boardroom. We won't be disturbed there."

Apparently Atticus wasn't allowed in the boardroom, because he jumped off the chair and trundled back to his spot under the reception desk, sighing loudly as he flumped his curly-haired body down onto the floor. I followed Leith into a long, windowless room with a mahogany table surrounded by several black leather swivel chairs. I selected a seat across from him and waited.

Leith placed the will in front of him, smoothing an invisible crease with a well-manicured hand, the nails showing evidence of a vigorous buffing. I wondered what kind of man went in for a mani-pedi—I was surmising on the pedi—and decided it was the kind of man who billed his services out for five hundred dollars an hour.

Unlike his office, which had a desk stacked high with paperwork, a saltwater aquarium, and walls covered with richly embroidered tapestries, the boardroom was devoid of clutter or ornamentation.

The sole exception was a framed photograph of an attractive blue-eyed blonde, mid-to-late twenties. She had her arms wrapped possessively around two fair-haired children, ages about three and five.

Mrs. Leith Hampton the fourth, I assumed, or possibly the fifth. I'd lost count, not that it mattered. My business here had nothing to do with Hampton's latest trophy wife or their gap-toothed offspring. I was here for the reading of my father's Last Will and Testament, an event I would have been far happier not attending for a good many years to come. Unfortunately, a faulty safety harness hadn't stopped his fall from the thirtieth floor of a condo under construction. The fact that a criminal defense attorney of Leith's reputation had drawn up the will was an indication of just how long the two men had been friends.

Leith cleared his throat and stared at me with those intense blue eyes. "Are you sure you're ready, Calamity? I know how close you were to your father."

I flinched at the Calamity. Folks called me Callie or they didn't call me at all. Only my dad had been allowed to call me Calamity, and even then only when he was seriously annoyed with me, and never in public. It was a deal we'd made back in elementary school. Kids can be cruel enough without the added incentive of a name like Calamity.

As for being ready, I'd been ready for the past ninety-plus minutes. I'd been ready since I first got the call telling me my father had been involved in an unfortunate occupational accident. That's how the detached voice on the other end of the phone had put it. *An unfortunate occupational accident.*

I knew at some point I'd have to face the fact that my dad wasn't coming back, that we'd never again argue over politics or share a laugh while watching an episode of *The Big Bang Theory*. Knew that one day I'd sit down and have a good long cry, but right now wasn't the time, and this certainly wasn't the place. I'd long ago learned to store my feelings into carefully constructed compartments. I leveled Leith with a dry-eyed stare and nodded.

"I'm ready."

Leith opened the file and began to read. "I, James David Barnstable, hereby declare that this is my last will and testament and that I hereby revoke, cancel, and annul all wills and codicils previously made by me either jointly or severally. I declare that I am of legal age to make this will and of sound mind and that this last will and testament expresses my wishes without undue influence or duress. I bequeath the whole of my estate, property, and effects, to my daughter, Calamity Doris Barnstable."

I nodded and tried to tune out the monotony of the will's legalese. I had expected no more and no less. I was the only child of two only children, and my mother had long ago left my dad and me to fend for ourselves. Not that the whole of his estate would amount to much; some well-worn furniture, a few mismatched dishes, and a small stack of dog-eared books, mostly Clive Cussler and Michael Connelly, with the occasional John Sandford tossed in for good measure.

The inheritance would mean clearing out my father's two-bedroom townhouse, a dreary example of 1970s architecture mired in the bowels of outer suburbia. I thought about my crammed studio apartment in downtown Toronto and knew that most of his belongings would wind up at the local Salvation Army or ReStore. The thought made me sad.

"There is one provision," Leith said, dragging me out of my reverie. "Your father wants you to move into the house in Marketville."

I sat up straighter and looked Leith in the eye. Clearly I'd missed something important when I'd zoned out. "What house in Marketville?"

Leith let out a theatrical courtroom sigh, well practiced but over the top for his audience of one. "You haven't really been listening, have you, Calamity?"

I was forced to admit I had not, although he now had my undivided attention. Marketville was a commuter community about an hour north of Toronto, the sort of town where families with two kids, a collie, and a cat moved to looking for a bigger house, a better school, and soccer fields. It didn't sound much like me, or my father.

"You're saying my father owned a house in Marketville? I don't understand. Why didn't he live there?"

Leith shrugged. "It seems he couldn't bear to part with it, and he couldn't stand living in it. He's been renting it out since 1986."

The year my mother had left. I'd been six. I tried to remember a house in Marketville. Nothing came to mind. Even my memories of my mother were vague.

"The house has gone through some hard times, what with tenants coming and going over the years," Leith continued. "I've done my best to manage the property for a modest monthly maintenance fee, but not living nearby…" He colored slightly and I wondered just how modest that fee had been. I glanced back at the photo of his vibrant young family and suspected such treasures did not come cheap. There was probably alimony for the other trophy wives as well. I decided to let it go. My father had trusted him. That had to be enough.

"So you're saying I've inherited a fixer-upper."

"I suppose you could put it that way, although your father had recently hired a company to make some basic improvements when the last tenant moved out." He flipped through his notes in the folder. "Royce Contracting and Property Management. I gather the owner of the company, Royce Ashford, lives next door. But I'm not sure much, if anything, has been done to the house yet. Naturally all work would have stopped following your father's death."

"You said he wanted me to move into the house? When was he going to tell me?"

"I think the initial plan was that your father was going to move back in there. But of course now—"

"Now that he's dead, you think he wanted me to move there?"

"Actually, it's more than wanted, Calamity. It's a provision of the will that you move into Sixteen Snapdragon Circle for a period of one year. After that time, you are free to do what you wish with it. Go back to renting it, continue to live there, or sell it."

"And if I decide to sell it?"

"Homes in that area of Marketville typically sell quickly and for a decent price, certainly several times your parents' original investment back in 1979. You'd have to put in some elbow grease, not to mention some basic renovations, but your father left you some money for that as well."

"He had money set aside? Enough for renovations?" I thought about the shabby townhouse, the threadbare carpets, the flannel sheet covering holes in the fabric of the ancient olive green brocade sofa. I always thought my dad was frugal because he had to be. It never occurred to me he was squirreling away money to fix up a house I didn't even know existed.

"About a hundred thousand dollars, although only half of that is allocated to renovation. The balance of fifty thousand would be paid to you in weekly installments while you lived there rent-free. Certainly enough for you to take a year off work and fulfill the other requirement."

Fifty thousand dollars. Almost twice what I made in a single year at my call center job at the bank. Leaving there would definitely not be a hardship. And my month-to-month lease would be easy enough to break with thirty days notice. "What's the other requirement?"

Leith leaned back in his chair and let out another one of his theatrical sighs. I got the impression he didn't really approve of the condition.

"Your father wants you to find out who murdered your mother. And he believes the clues may be hidden in the Marketville house."

2

______

I STARED at Leith Hampton open-mouthed. "What the hell are you talking about? My mother wasn't murdered. She left us when I was about six." I may not have had a clear recollection of my mother, but I still remembered the way kids talked about it at school, their parents the obvious source of information. Small town floozy finds a new man and makes tracks for a better life. Until now I had no idea the gossip had surfaced anywhere other than Toronto.

"Apparently your father came to believe otherwise," Leith said, folding his arms in front of his chest.

This surprised me. My mother's name was seldom mentioned when I was growing up. Most of the time it felt as if she'd never existed. My natural curiosity about who she was and where she went had been far from sated. The few things my father told me about her, usually after a couple of beers, hardly counted. That her name was Abigail; that she liked to bake; that she loved old movies, especially musicals from the 1950s.

"So you're saying the Marketville house never used to be part of his will?"

"The house was always part of the will, and you were always the beneficiary. The codicil is the part where you have to go live in the house for a year and try to solve your mother's alleged murder, or failing that, discover the real reason behind her disappearance." Leith shook his head. "I'll admit I didn't support the idea, but he insisted. I did my best to talk him out of it, but you know how obstinate your father could be."

I did. Look up stubborn in the dictionary and you might just find a picture of James David Barnstable. It was a trait I had inherited, right along with his unruly mop of chestnut brown hair and black-rimmed hazel eyes. The hair I could straighten into submission, given enough product and enough patience with a blow dryer and flat iron, and the eyes were probably my best feature. But the stubborn streak had almost proved my undoing on more than one occasion. My father's, too. "Do you know what led to his fixation?"

"I know he hired a private investigator when your mother first left, but nothing came of it. It was as if she'd vanished into thin air. There may have been some other attempts that I'm not aware of. But it was his last tenant in the Marketville house that reignited the fire."

"How so?"

Leith gave a dry chuckle, but there was no humor in the sound. "Apparently the tenant was a psychic, or at least she claimed to be. A woman by the name of Misty Rivers."

As someone named after Calamity Jane, a Wild West frontierswoman of questionable repute, I wasn't about to criticize anyone else's moniker. I was just grateful my parents had the good sense to give me a different middle name. "What did this Misty Rivers do or say to get my father's attention?"

"She told him the house was haunted by someone who once lived there, someone who loved lilacs."

"And from that he reached the conclusion my mother had been murdered?"

"It's a reach, I know. But in the past another tenant had complained of weird noises. Creaking in the basement, footsteps in the attic, that sort of thing. We both dismissed the complaint as the tenant's attempt to get out of her lease. If that was the objective, it worked. She moved out early without paying a penalty."

"But then after the psychic—"

"Exactly. After Misty Rivers, your father wasn't so sure. When you moved out of the Marketville house, he'd locked up all of your mother's things in the attic. He said he couldn't bear to go through them after she left, then the years just ticked on by. Misty made him believe there might be clues hidden amongst your mother's belongings."

It was as if Leith was talking about a stranger. "He never told me about any of this."

"He wanted to be sure, to protect you from getting hurt. He didn't want you believing in what might only have been a fairy tale."

A fairy tale. Except this one didn't seem to have a happy ending. I fished around in my purse for my cocoa butter lip balm while I thought about it.

"What's all this about lilacs?"

"Over the years, folks have tried planting a variety of things, flowers, a vegetable garden, all without any measure of success. The only thing that grew on the property was an out-of-control lilac bush in the backyard. It didn't matter how many times it was cut back, the following spring it would come back full and bushy. Apparently your mother had planted it."

I rolled my eyes. "Lilacs are known for their indestructibility. And it would be easy enough for someone to see an old lilac bush and draw the conclusion the original owner had planted it." Another thought occurred to me. "This Misty Rivers, did she want money?"

Leith nodded, his expression grave. "I believe your father was going to pay her to investigate. Against my advice, speaking on the record. Unfortunately for Ms. Rivers, his premature death intervened."

Unbelievable. My common sense, union dues paying, hardworking tradesman of a father. Hiring a psychic. What had he been thinking?

It was as if Leith Hampton had read my mind. "I know it's a lot to take in, Callie. All I know is that in the past few months, your father became increasingly obsessed with your mother's… disappearance. I have to admit that I didn't see it coming. All these years, he refused to talk about her, and for good reason."

"What good reason?"

Leith clamped his lips together as if he wanted to bite back the words he said, or was going to say.

"What good reason, Leith?" I asked, again. "If I'm going off on this wild goose chase, at the very least I need to know everything there is to know."

Leith sighed, but there were no theatrics this time. "I suppose you're right, and besides, once you get digging into the past, you're bound to find out."

I know lawyers get paid by the hour but there was no need to drag this on. I leaned forward, standing semi upright while my fingernails tapped on the polished mahogany surface. "Bound to find out what?"

"Although your mother's body was never found, no one ever saw or heard from her again. The police suspected foul play. Although your father was the one who reported her missing, he soon became the prime suspect. There was a lot of neighborhood gossip."

"Because the spouse is always the first one police suspect," I said, thinking of the countless episodes of *Law and Order* I'd seen over the years.

"Exactly. Eventually, the police moved on, but the case was never closed. The damage it did to your father's reputation in Marketville…he just couldn't stay there. He also couldn't bear to sell the home. Hence, the rentals over the years."

"And going back now? Revisiting ancient history, opening old wounds. What was he hoping to prove?"

Leith shrugged. "Maybe he just wanted to clear his name, Calamity. Maybe adding the codicil was his way of asking you to do the same. I wish he'd confided in me more than he did. When it came to his legal matters, he didn't treat me as a friend, he treated me as his lawyer. I encouraged that view of our relationship."

"I work at a bank call center. The only thing I know how to

investigate is customer complaints." I tried to process everything Leith had told me. "You said I needed to move into the house. What if I don't find out anything?" What if, as was entirely likely, there was nothing to find out? What if I found evidence that implicated my father?

"Your only obligation is to try, and of course, to live there."

"If I don't want to?"

"Fifty thousand dollars would be held in escrow for renovations. Misty Rivers would be allowed to live in the Marketville house, rent-free for the period of one year, with the proviso she investigates your mother's disappearance. I would be given weekly progress reports, for which she would be paid one thousand dollars per report. The same sort of progress reports you would be expected to give, should you agree to take this on. The entire fifty thousand dollars would be paid outright should the mystery of your mother's disappearance be solved before the year was up."

Weekly progress reports saying what? The lilac was back in bloom? I wanted to scream. Instead I asked, "What happens after a year?"

"Misty Rivers moves out. The house will come into your full possession, to do with what you like. No more strings."

In the meantime, some swindling psychic would be pawing through my mother's belongings and living rent-free, probably without any interest in clearing my father's name. Not on my dime and not on my time.

"As I mentioned earlier, your obligation ceases one year from the date you move in. After that, you're free to do what you wish. Sell the house, continue to live there, put it back on the rental market. The fifty thousand dollars for renovations would be available from the moment you move in. Any dollars not used for renovations will come to you free and clear."

"And what becomes of Misty Rivers?

"She's on a five-thousand dollar retainer, should you decide to consult with her." I couldn't imagine doing any such a thing.

But it looked as if I was moving to Marketville.

3

―――――

Snapdragon Circle was a cul-de-sac within an enclave of 1970s bungalows, split-levels, and semis. The occasional two-story home dotted an otherwise predictable suburban landscape, although closer inspection revealed upper level additions to the original structures.

Every road within the subdivision had been named after a provincial wildflower, starting with the central artery of Trillium Way and branching out to symmetrical side streets with names like Day Lily Drive, Lady's Slipper Lane, and Coneflower Crescent.

Most of the homes appeared to be well cared for, the lawns lush and green, the windows gleaming. Sixteen Snapdragon Circle, a yellow brick bungalow with a badly sagging carport, was the one notable exception. The roof had been patched in a half dozen places with little attention paid to attempting a match in the color of the shingles. The windows were caked with years of dirt and grit, and quite possibly, a few eggs from Halloweens past.

To say the house needed a little bit of TLC was putting a gloss on things. What this house needed was a good coat of fire.

It took me a minute to realize that a man had wandered over to the bare scratch of front lawn to join me. I pegged him to be about forty, good looking in a rugged handyman sort of way, the kind of guy you'd see on one of those TV home improvement shows. Well-defined biceps, sandy brown hair cropped close to his scalp, warm brown eyes. He wore jeans, work boots, and a black golf shirt with a gold logo advertising Royce Contracting & Property Maintenance. I imagined a six-pack under that shirt and tried hard not to blush.

"Royce Ashford," he said, extending his right hand. "I live next door." He gestured to an immaculate back-split, gray brick with white vinyl siding. The siding looked new.

So this was the contractor Leith Hampton had mentioned—the contractor my dad had hired.

"Callie Barnstable."

"Are you the new tenant?" There was something in the way he said it, a hint of "here we go again" and "poor you" implicit in the words.

"Even worse. I own this place. Quit my job to move here."

For a brief moment, Royce raised his eyebrows in surprise, but he recovered quickly. "I heard about his accident. I'm sorry. He seemed like a good man."

"Thank you. I understood from Leith Hampton—my father's lawyer—that you knew my father."

"I wouldn't say I knew him, exactly. I met him for the first time a few weeks ago. I gather he hadn't been here in a few years—all the rentals were handled through Hampton & Associates. He seemed quite shocked at the state of disrepair." Royce smiled. "I'm afraid tenants don't always respect a property the way they might if it was their own."

"I noticed."

"Your dad was planning to renovate. I'd given him a few ideas and an estimate. I got the impression he was planning to move back in."

So Leith had been right, my father had planned to come back to Marketville. I wondered if he had planned to sell the townhouse. I thought about the postcards from realtors addressed to "The Estate of James David Barnstable" that I'd tossed in the trash. I was definitely going to sell the townhouse once probate cleared, but I wasn't about to list it with someone so tactless. Now I wondered if any one of those realtors had talked to my father. I heard Royce clear his throat and realized he'd been talking to me.

"I'm sorry, I was off in my own world."

"I expect it's all a bit overwhelming for you. I was saying that you're free to find another contractor. Whatever you decide, I'd suggest getting the roof re-shingled before you get leaks inside the house. Your father had already gotten quotes and selected a company. I could set that up for you, if you'd like."

"Thank you, that would be great. The sooner the better, from the looks of things. I'd also like to discuss the rest of the renovations once I get settled in." I just hoped it wouldn't take up the entire fifty thousand dollars. Leith had mentioned that whatever was left over would come to me. It could buy me a little more time to figure out what I was going to do once my year was up. I couldn't imagine going back to the call center.

"I'll see how soon I can get the roofers in. As for the other renos, there's no rush. You can let me know when you're ready. In the meantime, if you're up for a drink or dinner—no obligation to discuss business—let me know. It can't be easy coming to a town where you don't know anyone."

"Thank you." I pulled out my cocoa lip balm, dabbed a bit on my lips, and wondered about the best way to approach Royce. I decided to go full at it. "Do you mind if I ask you something?"

"Not at all. Ask away."

"Did you happen to know the last tenant?"

A slow grin spread across Royce's face. "I assume you mean Misty Rivers, psychic extraordinaire. She was convinced the house was haunted, tried to convince your father of the same."

Just as I had suspected. It wasn't just *I think it's haunted*. The woman had done her best to mess with my father's head, and it seemed to have worked, although why he had believed her was another matter entirely.

"Do you believe in such things?" I studied Royce through narrowed eyes.

"I'll tell you the same thing I told your dad," Royce said, shrugging his shoulders. "I was born and raised in Marketville, and in the late 1970s, the population would have been roughly 20,000, less than a quarter of what it has today. These houses were built to entice first time homeowners with young families. Folks who couldn't afford to buy in the city. Back then the building code wasn't as stringent as it is today, and to be fair, a lot of the technology and energy efficiencies that we now take for granted hadn't even been developed. Add to the mix that the house has been tenanted for thirty years, with minimal attention paid to upkeep, and there's bound to be some squeaks and squawks."

"So the short answer is no."

That slow grin appeared once again.

"I suppose, Callie, that you're about to find out."

4

———

The inside of Sixteen Snapdragon Circle wasn't much better than the outside. I went around the house, opening the windows to get rid of a musty smell that seemed to infuse every room. Then I went back to the entrance and took stock of my inheritance.

Avocado green and gold linoleum flooring in the hallway carried through to a small eat-in kitchen, the cupboards painted a gloss chocolate brown, the walls sunshine yellow. Harvest gold appliances. A laminate countertop, gold speckles on off-white, a pot ring burned into its scarred surface. A window over the sink overlooked the sagging carport. Welcome back, 1980.

An old memory came to mind. Me, as a little girl, four, maybe five years old, curly brown hair in a messy bob, standing on a footstool and staring out of that very same window. I was wearing a red and white striped apron with tiny heart-shaped pockets. I used to hide tiny pieces of beef liver in those pockets so I could flush the bits down the toilet after dinner. My parents had a strict "eat your dinner or there's no dessert" policy, and no amount of gravy or fried onions made the liver tolerable to my taste buds.

I closed my eyes, hoping to remember more.

Popped them wide open when I heard a creak in the attic.

A shiver ran through me. I found the furnace control and turned up the heat. To the left of the hallway was a combination living room-dining room. I wondered if there was hardwood underneath the threadbare gold carpet that covered the floor. I knelt down, lifted up a heat vent, and pulled back a corner to reveal a strip of pale blonde hardwood. Small mercies. That rug's days were seriously numbered, and stripping carpet was something I could do myself. It would save a bit of renovation money for another project. From the looks of this place, fifty thousand dollars wasn't going to go far. If I wanted to sell in a year and get a decent amount for the place, I'd have to put in a lot of elbow grease.

Another hallway led out of the kitchen and dining room and into a main bathroom in shades of 1970s pink, and two bedrooms painted builder's beige. The smaller room was barely larger than a walk-in closet; the master bedroom was just large enough to fit a queen-sized bed if you were the kind of person who didn't care about night tables. The eyesore of a rug continued throughout. I lifted up another heat vent and found evidence of more pale blonde hardwood.

Both bedrooms had decent-sized windows, with the master affording a view of the backyard. I noticed the sprawling lilac, not yet in bud. It was early May after an unseasonably harsh winter. It could be at least another month before it would be in full bloom.

I opened the master bedroom closet and made note of a small footstool and attic entry. According to Leith, my mother's things would be stored there. I wasn't looking forward to rummaging around an attic—thoughts of mouse poop and spider webs sprang to mind, and I really hated closed-in spaces—but it would have to be done, and sooner rather than later. If I could solve this supposed "mystery" or prove there was no mystery to solve, I could go back to my life in downtown Toronto. It might not have been exciting, but it was cloaked in anonymity, something the recluse in me relished. Five years in my condo rental, I had yet to get to know any of my neighbors. One hour in Marketville and my neighbor had already invited me over for a drink or dinner.

I continued with my investigation of the house. A narrow

stairway led to the basement. I'm not a huge fan of basements. They always feel vaguely creepy to me, and the low ceilings and dark wood paneling did nothing to warm me to this one. There was a separate room with an ancient washer and dryer not long for this world. It wasn't a wringer washer, but it wasn't far off. A second room housed the furnace, original to the house from the looks of it. It would probably need to be replaced before next winter. I mentally tallied up the renovation expenses I'd made note of so far and tried to shake off a feeling of gloom. It looked like I had inherited a money pit, and maybe a haunted one at that.

As if on cue, the furnace made a strange, belching noise before shuddering into submission.

"I hear you," I said, and scampered up the stairs, taking them two steps at a time.

ABOUT THE AUTHOR

A former journalist and magazine editor, Judy Penz Sheluk is the author of two mystery series: the Glass Dolphin Mysteries and the Marketville Mysteries. Her short crime fiction appears in several collections, including *The Best Laid Plans* and *Heartbreaks & Half-truths*, which she also edited.

Judy is a member of Sisters in Crime, International Thriller Writers, the Short Mystery Fiction Society, and Crime Writers of Canada, where she serves as Chair on the Board of Directors. Find her at judypenzsheluk.com.

9 781989 495278